The Museum Murders

A mystery novel by
Tim Kelly

Circa 1959
©2009

Published in the USA by:
BearManor Media
P O Box 71426
Albany, Georgia 31708
www.bearmanormedia.com

ISBN 1-59393-353-3

Printed in the United States of America.

Book and cover design by Darlene and Dan Swanson of Van-garde Imagery, Inc.

An Introduction

You are holding in your hands something rare and wonderful. It is a novel written a half century ago by Vera S. Morris, the preferred pseudonym of the late Tim Kelly.

While researching and writing the authorized biography, *Tim Kelly: Master of Stage Fright* (BearManor Media, 2009), I was permitted unprecedented access to the works, both published and unpublished, of this man I so admire. He was the successful author of countless musicals, one-acts and melodramas—many of which are still being performed in high schools and colleges. True, he did write a few novels, including at least one mass-produced western titled *Ride of Fury*, but Mr. Kelly was first and foremost a dramatist. He was drawn to the activity and spirit and daring that can only be provided by living people courageously showing themselves on a stage.

Tim Kelly was a superb craftsman, cleverly constructing vehicles for his core audience of students. In reading this heretofore unreleased novel (originally titled "Paint Me a Murder"), one is reminded of his playwriting prowess. *The Museum Murders* offers clearly established situations, unexpected twists, colorful characters, and an abundance of crisp, witty dialogue. What it does *not* have is explicit sex or violence—in the tradition of classic mystery novels, those elements are merely implied. It is, in a sense, a period piece. The action

3

takes place in the arts scene of Mr. Kelly's adopted town, Phoenix, Arizona, in the late 1950s—a time when that now-thriving metropolis was still a comparatively undeveloped desert community searching for its cultural identity.

It is an honor to provide a rare glimpse of Tim Kelly the novelist in the *genre* he liked best—the mystery. I hope you enjoy reading a different side of America's most prolific playwright.

Ben Ohmart

BearManor Media

Summer 2008

Chapter One

"You must see the Waddington. It'll scare you half to death."

They pushed their way through the crowd and stood in front of the canvas.

Charlie was intrigued; Dolly less so.

"Well," asked Lisa anxiously, "what do you think?"

"I'm not really sure," said Dolly softly. "Rather unnerving, isn't it?"

"That's what makes Waddington's work delicious."

Lisa was hoping her friends would like the painting, and this was obvious to Charlie. He began to study the work closely.

The colors were oddly muted. The technique unorthodox, but there was no denying the artist was skilled. The subject matter, however, made the creation unforgettable, at least in Charlie's eyes; showing in the distance a landscape of desert mountains hinting at gloom. The center attraction was the depiction of a ghost town cemetery. Five graves. Bouquets of roses and thorny sagebrush were intertwined around each of the five wooden crosses. A desolate cottonwood tree, charred and ominous, stood obscenely as the focal point. The creation was entitled: "Happing Landings!"

Charlie and Dolly exchanged uncertain glances.

Hesitatingly, Dolly began to give her honest opinion, but Lisa cut her off.

"Come on," she gushed, grabbing Dolly's hand, "I see Wadding-ton over by the stairwell."

Lisa led them through the mob.

"Isn't going to be like this every day!" she exclaimed, shouting to make herself heard. "Looks like everyone in town has showed for the opening."

"What?"

"Everyone—everyone in town has showed ..."

Dolly made a sign meaning she couldn't hear her friend over the hubbub. Lisa nodded, understanding.

Now they were at the stairwell, and Lisa managed to pull Wad-dington into a nearby alcove.

"Easier to talk here."

"Yes, yes," said Waddington quickly.

Lars Waddington was a large man, but arthritis had robbed him of good posture, and he was obliged to lean heavily on his cane of brightly-colored Mexican design. His hair was totally white and thinning fast, and although the muscles of his lean face were tight, the expression cast was pleasant enough. Charlie surmised the artist was in his sixties.

"This is my best friend," Lisa beamed, taking Dolly's arm. "She and I were in show business together. Years ago."

"Three years at most," Dolly corrected.

Lisa giggled, then drawled formally, "Mr. and Mrs. Underwood, may I present Mr. Waddington."

The artist held out his hand in greeting. "Lars."

Charlie shook his hand, returning with: "Charlie. My wife goes by Dolly."

"Dolly? Odd name. Don't think I've ever met a Dolly."

"Charlie and Dolly will be here for several weeks. Escaping the New Hampshire winter."

"How do you find Arizona?" the artist asked.

"We haven't seen much of it, actually," answered Charlie.

Dolly said, "We just got in yesterday. Barely got unpacked and Lisa was on the phone telling us about the new museum."

"Yes, yes, marvelous. Our first museum. 'Course we always had a museum. But it was a rundown stable. Nothing more. Phoenix is growing. Must have a museum. Modern, rich, active."

"I'd say the opening was a tremendous success."

"Every opening's a success, Charlie. But we'll do well, I'm confident." He turned slowly, facing Lisa. "Your friends will be here for the wedding, then?"

"They'd better be. Have you seen my future husband about?"

"I believe he went to fetch Gina."

"Oh."

Lisa was visibly annoyed.

"Gina said she might not come, you know," Lars added.

"No, I didn't know."

"That's Gina Langley," he said by way of explanation.

"The authoress?" asked Dolly, rather surprised.

"Yes," Lisa cut in, "among other things."

The museum was officially named Langley Memorial Art Museum. Dolly was curious about the connection. One obviously existed between the new building and the famed Gina Langley.

"I didn't know she lived in Phoenix," said Charlie.

"In the winter," Lars replied.

"Haven't heard her name for some time. She doesn't write anymore, does she?"

"Not the sort of thing she once did."

"Got religion, didn't she?"

Charlie felt a slight kick to the shin from Dolly.

"I found your painting fascinating, Lars."

"Did you? Which one?"

"'Happy Landings.'"

"Yes, that is good. That cemetery exists. Outside of Jerome. A mile down from the Cleopatra mine. That would make an interesting side trip for you two—Jerome. Whole place is a ghost town. I have two other paintings on exhibit. You must see them."

"Oh, I intend to. May I ask you a question, Lars?"

"Go ahead."

"How do you explain it?"

"Explain what?"

"Your painting. 'Happy Landings.'"

"Good heavens, Mrs. Underwood, if I could explain it, I wouldn't have to paint it. Ah, here he is, Lisa—your young man."

Michael Jarvits was a wiry individual, with close-cropped blond hair and large dark eyes that made his face seem smaller than it was. He was accompanied by the museum's director.

"Hi!" he said boyishly.

"Hi," replied Lisa, with an air of indifference.

"See, you're meeting one of our more famous Valley artists."

"Yes, indeed," said Dolly.

"We were looking for you earlier," Charlie said.

"Had to attend to a few things."

Charlie half-expected Lisa to say something, but she was busily studying the crowd.

"Charlie and Dolly, I'd like to have you meet the museum's director. Howard Stacey."

Mr. Stacey shook hands with the Underwoods. He was a thick-figured man and appeared to lack a neck, but he was jovial and solicitous, speaking in a flat midwestern dialect.

"My assistant here, Michael, tells me you're in police work, Mr. Underwood."

"After a fashion."

"Hope it's not business that brings you out this way."

"We're here on a holiday," contributed Dolly.

"You'll find Arizona a wonderful place for that. Lot warmer than in the East."

"New Hampshire winters can be lovely. But Charlie and I thought we'd like to see something of the New West."

"Splendid. Phoenix is the place for that."

"Congratulations on the museum," Charlie smiled. "Must give you quite a sense of accomplishment."

"Yes."

A dwarfish man with thick glasses was standing beside Michael. He interrupted the conversation with a curt, "Have you spoken with Gina?"

Michael turned and said sharply, "Yes. I'll talk to you later."

"*Now.*"

"I can't talk now."

"I insist."

An expression of annoyance mapped Michael's face.

"Very well," he snapped. He excused himself and left the alcove.

"That was Hank Ullman," volunteered Lisa. "The little fella. He's attorney for the museum."

"May I get you ladies some punch?" asked Stacey.

"I'd love some," Dolly responded, "but can you fight your way through that mob?"

"We can try," said Charlie. "I'd better help you, Howard. Juggling cups of punch through that mass might not be easy."

"Come along then."

They began the journey to a buffet set up at the extreme end of the room.

"You have an exceptional collection to start the museum off," Charlie said, hitting the first wave of milling people.

"Once the museum has Gina's Utrillo collection—"

"What?"

"I said, 'once the museum has the Utrillo—'"

"Better wait until we're at the punchbowl."

Howard laughed and pushed on.

Lars Waddington was drawn from the alcove by a bevy of admirers, and Dolly and Lisa sat wearily on a marble bench.

"Never thought marble would feel so good," sighed Lisa.

"You were here early this morning, weren't you?"

"Dolly, please don't remind me. I'm with the Lady Boosters." Dolly laughed.

"Now you're being superior."

"I'm not. Really, I'm not. But I can't conceive of you as a Lady Booster."

"A year ago I would have agreed. But a year ago I didn't know Mike. That's the difference."

"Mike and Lisa Jarvits. Go back in showbiz with a team name like that."

"No, thank you. If my feet are going to hurt let it be because I'm a Lady Booster, not a Lady Hoofer. Believe me, this is only the beginning."

"Yes, I imagine as wife of the assistant director, your job's cut out for you."

"Oh, I don't mind. I'm anxious to get on with the business of being a wife. Odd, though, when you stop to think about it. I was certain we'd stay in New York—with a museum there. Then this position opened and—well—frankly, it was too good to pass up."

"You did the right thing, I'm sure."

"You know how it is back East, Dolly. Out here there's a chance to get ahead. In a New York museum, Mike would have to wait a century for the chance at a directorship, but out here—I mean, well— Howard Stacey isn't going to live forever, is he?"

Lisa had previously kicked off her shoes. Now she put them back on, chattering as she did so. Dolly was half-listening. Lisa's last remark about Stacey not living forever struck her as peculiar.

Shoes on, Lisa took Dolly's hands in hers.

"I can't tell you how delighted I am you're here, Dolly. Going to be my maid of honor, too. Married on my twenty-third birthday—isn't that something? I'll never forget my wedding anniversary, will I? My birthday coming on the same day and all."

Dolly gave out with a wry grin.

"Why are you playing the Cheshire?"

"You're going to be married on *what* birthday?"

"My twenty-third. You're still grinning."

"When we were dancing in that off-Broadway thing—"

"*Leave It to Jane.*"

"You were eighteen months older than I and—Lisa, I'm pushing twenty-five."

Lisa rose quickly.

"No need to make that sound like candidacy for Forest Lawn."

They looked at one another for a moment, silently, trying not to burst into laughter. They failed.

Dolly stopped laughing when she noticed a commotion taking place by an exhibit of Rodin castings.

"That's Mike, isn't it?"

"Where?"

"By the Rodins."

Mike and Ullman were arguing heatedly. People were beginning to notice. The little man was red in the face; Mike was trying to get away from him, but with no success.

"Here's the punch," piped Charlie, coming back into the alcove. "Or rather what's left of it. Started out with full cups, like good intentions—"

Stacey was close behind, holding a cup of punch in each hand.

"Howard," Lisa said nervously. "I think there's some trouble." She indicated the two men by the statuary.

"Isn't that Michael?"

"Yes," snapped Lisa.

"Isn't that Hank Ullman with him?"

"Yes."

"What's happening?"

Lisa's patience was giving out.

"I don't know, Howard—that's why I mentioned it to you."

"I'd better see what this is all about."

Hastily, he thrust two glass cups into Dolly's hands and hurried in the direction of the arguers.

"Hank has a temper," Lisa sighed.

Because he could think of nothing any less foolish, Charlie said, "Hope it's not serious."

People cleared a path for Stacey. He reached the men. The Underwoods could see Mike nodding and agreeing, although Ullman showed no signs of calming down. Finally, Stacey was able to separate them and he headed back to the alcove with Mike.

"I think you could use this," said Charlie with a sympathetic smile. Mike took the offered drink and downed it in one pull.

"Thanks."

"Is everything alright?" asked Lisa.

"You know how Hank can be when he thinks someone's going over his head."

"Awkward," muttered Stacey. "The opening and all."

"Hardly anyone noticed," Dolly lied.

Both Charlie and Dolly were curious about what had transpired, but tension was in the air, so they postponed their questions.

For some time the five people in the alcove said nothing in the way of conversation. Michael was depressed; Lisa worried. Then his mood swiftly reversed itself and he brightened.

"Ah, there's Carter Aubery. Said he wasn't coming. I knew he'd change his mind. If you'll excuse me."

The Underwoods stammered, "Of course."

Lisa attempted to pick up on her fiancé's lighter mood.

"You must meet Carter. He puts out *Arrowheads*."

"*Arrowheads*?" repeated Dolly as a question.

Howard Stacey supplied explanation, "Our city magazine. Quite nice. Only two years old. An infant. You'll have to get used to that. Everything in this town is new."

A Lady Booster in a thick black dress, decorated with an enormous corsage of camellia, was waving to him by a casting of Rodin's "The Kiss." Howard returned the wave and fought his way toward her.

"Really," said Lisa in exasperation, "you'd think Howard would do something about the way he dresses."

Actually, Charlie and Dolly had already noted Stacey's attire. His suit was outdated and tweedy, his shirt checkered, and in rather violent contrast he fancied a hand-painted necktie displaying the joys of forest conservation, complete with a woodland fawn drinking from a brook.

"This isn't a one-horse town anymore," shot Lisa. "That sort of garb might have been fine when the museum was in a stable. Not anymore. I wouldn't be surprised if Mike wasn't forced to give him a few tips in the sartorial department."

She had spoken with such confidence that Dolly was first stunned, then amused.

"And how long, Miss Lady Booster, have you been living here?"

"Almost three months."

"You've become something of an authority in three months, haven't you?"

"I know what's going on, anyway. Oh, there are a few people connected with the museum who aren't much better than crumbs held together by their dough, but most are nice. I mean, well, the museum *is* reaching for something in the class department, and I think the director should be a bit more—"

"Classy?" Charlie suggested.

"Exactly," countered Lisa, and Charlie felt another stab at his shinbone.

The next hour moved uneventfully. There was no doubt that the opening of the new museum was a smash, yet it had a considerable drawback, for as the afternoon wore on, the number of people who pressed into the reception made viewing the displayed works virtually impossible.

"And I wanted to see the other Waddingtons."

"We can make another trip, Dolly. When the crowd isn't here."

"Oh, we don't have to come here to see his works, Charlie."

"How so?"

"Lars has invited us to his place. Says that's the only way to see them. In quiet."

"When did this happen?"

"While you were fetching the punch, love."

"I don't intend to run that course again—it would take a fullback. What do you say? Had enough?"

"I think we should say goodbye to Lisa and Mike."

"Haven't seen either one in the last half hour."

It came from the direction of the castings. No one paid much attention until it was repeated. There could be no doubt that someone was screaming. This was followed by general confusion and a frantic push by the mob, uncertain of itself.

"What is it?" Dolly cried out.

People had begun to pull back from the area devoted to the castings, and two museum guards moved in quickly. Charlie was behind them.

Howard Stacey was down on one knee, examining the body.

A woman shouted, "Isn't someone going to get a doctor? Why doesn't someone send for a doctor?"

"We'll take care of this," a guard retorted. "Keep back, keep back."

A magnificent bronze had toppled from its anchoring on a fairly high pedestal: a figure sitting with arms outstretched, head bent low.

Stacey was shaking his head slowly from side to side, indicating that the man was dead. Charlie craned his neck to see, but he couldn't make out the identity of the deceased.

"I was talking to him a moment ago," a woman stuttered to the guard.

Charlie saw Mike Jarvits head for the phone on the reception desk. People were asking questions, angrily.

"How could it have fallen?"

"Where was he standing?"

"It was unsafe—the pedestal."

And again, almost desperately: "How could it have fallen?"

Stacey turned the man over. Charlie instinctively wanted to protest, but kept his silence. It was the museum's lawyer, Hank Ullman.

"Just a moment ago," a near-hysterical woman was whining, "poor Hank said he couldn't stay. He had an appointment."

He *had* an appointment alright, Charlie thought to himself—with a gentleman named Rodin.

Chapter Two

Charlie rose early the following morning. Sleep hadn't come easy, so as soon as dawn broke he was up and out for the papers.

They were staying at a large resort motel-hotel, Mountain Shadows, not far from Phoenix. Rooms were cabana-styled and edged the ring of an enormous swimming pool. He drove into town and found a drugstore open with the morning papers stacked high on the soda fountain. He purchased a *Journal* and a *Republic*. Each devoted considerable front-page space to the grisly mishap.

When he returned to Mountain Shadows, there were signs of activity on the part of the staff, and he was able to have a pot of coffee sent to his cabana. In front of each cabana a ramada stretched out toward the pool and beneath its shade, chaise lounges, bamboo chairs and side tables made for something of a tropical sitting room.

Dolly was still deep in sleep when he got back. He peeked in and studied her sleeping form. She was on her side, her cheek resting against her hands which she had slipped between the pillow and her head. Her blonde hair stood out shiningly in the darkened room. In her sleep she had tossed back the blanket, and her body, trim and full, was perfectly relaxed. He thought of waking her with a kiss but decided against it. She was something of a tiger when disturbed from a nap or night's rest.

Over several cups of coffee, Charlie read the news coverage. The *Journal* first:

NOTED PHOENIX LAWYER
DEAD IN FREAK MISHAP

Henry Lester Ullman, distinguished Phoenix attorney, was pronounced dead-on-arrival at St. Joseph Hospital, following a bizarre mishap at yesterday's opening of the new $1,000,000 Langley Memorial Art Museum.

Ullman, attorney for many prominent Phoenicians as well as the museum, was killed instantly when a bronze casting of Rodin's "Sorrow" toppled from its pedestal and struck him on the right temple.

Police are questioning several people who were standing close to Ullman when the incident occurred, although no names have been revealed.

Ullman was a bachelor with no known survivors as far as the *Journal* has been able to ascertain.

A coroner's inquiry is imminent.

Museum director Howard Stacey said the bronze casting was valued at $2,800.

(More on Ullman, pg. 16)

The *Republic* front-page blurb was basically the same, but it (for some reason incomprehensible to Charlie) stressed the deceased's political affiliations, highlighting the fact that Ullman had once headed a "Drive-Taft-For-The-Presidency" campaign.

The deceased's photograph showed a dour-looking individual.

Eyeglasses took up most of the upper half of his uninteresting face and looked as thick as the bottom of pop bottles.

Charlie read related columns, including a society splash that reveled in the new museum.

A young woman, long-limbed and voluptuous, left her nearby cabana for a morning plunge when Charlie distinctly heard the sound of a meow.

The lovely creature wasn't in a bikini; in fact, Charlie wasn't certain what it was. Leopard was the swimsuit's motif, but it had a wonderful shimmering quality to its two scant pieces.

She dipped her toes in the water and made circles on the top of the water with one foot.

"Go on in," urged Charlie.

She looked up and glanced at him with an ingratiating smile.

"To-o-o cold."

Her voice was deep and a touch hoarse, reminding him of Margaret Sullavan, his favorite film star when he was a boy.

"Don't think about it. Jump right in."

He was beaming at her. The sound of meowing passed unnoticed.

"I don't swim very well. Perhaps I'll drown."

"Oh, you won't drown."

"But the lifeguard doesn't come on duty until ten." She pointed to a sign that proved her correct.

"Pretend *I'm* the lifeguard. Jump in."

"Alright," she said spontaneously, "but only because you're here."

She dove in, hitting the water neatly. Charlie could see she was a fine swimmer in spite of her playfulness. Her underwater scissor kick was perfect.

"*Meow.*"

Turning, he saw Dolly standing in the doorway.

"Oh, oh, it's you, baby."

"Who did you expect to find climbing out of your bed?"

He laughed—sort of.

"I've been meowing for the last five minutes."

Meowing when she awoke was a Dolly Underwood routine. When they were first married and traveling through Europe on a six-week honeymoon tour, Charlie remarked that she stretched like a cat. The following morning she woke her young husband by meowing and clawing at his naked back. (Charlie disliked tops.) After that it became something of a morning ritual. The meowing, not the clawing.

"I've been reading about Ullman."

"So I noticed."

The leopard woman finished her dip, climbed out of the pool, and strode gracefully along the poolwalk and into her cabana, tossing a teasing smile over her shoulder at Charlie.

He swallowed hard.

"Little early in the morning for you to be playing Frank Buck*, isn't it?"

He started to protest, but Dolly yawned loudly, and snatched away the papers, retreating back to the bed.

An hour later, finished with coffee and the papers, the Underwoods were preparing to go to town. Dolly wanted to do some shopping and see Lisa.

The shopping apparently could wait; Lisa could not.

She was standing outside the cabana's large picture window, tapping on the pane. Dolly went to the door and opened it wide.

"For goodness sake, Lisa—what brings you out here? I thought we were all going to meet for lunch."

"We will, we will," she said breathily, and then swept past Dolly and seated herself in an armchair by the bed. "Close the door."

"Lisa, I don't understand—"

"Please."

---

* Frank Buck (1884-1950) was a famous hunter and "collector of wild animals." He appeared in the Ringling Bros. Barnum & Bailey Circus and co-authored the 1930 best-seller, *Bring 'Em Back Alive*.

Dolly did as she was asked.

Lisa was in a state. Rarely did she appear *anywhere* looking less than stunning, but this morning she wore no makeup and had thrown a dark cloth coat, much too warm for the day, over her shoulders. She fumbled in her purse for cigarettes, couldn't locate any and sighed in disgust.

Charlie came to her rescue, and lighted the cigarette she took from his pack of filter-tips. Lisa took a deep drag, settling back in the chair.

"You want a drink?" said Charlie.

"No, no, I'll be myself in a moment."

She took a few more puffs on the cigarette, then nervously tapped it out in a stand ashtray.

To Charlie, she implored: "I need your help."

"In what way?"

"You've read the papers." She nodded at the papers which were spread out on the bed.

"You mean about Ullman."

She nodded yes.

"I wish I could tell you what it is that I want you to do, Charlie, but I can't. I mean, I'm not certain I know." She was annoyed with herself. "That is—"

"Why don't you relax?" coaxed Charlie.

"Let me take your coat," Dolly said.

Lisa slipped it off and handed it to her.

"Don't know why I put on the damn thing. Never need a coat in weather like this. In the morning."

"Is it about Mike?" Charlie queried.

"Yes."

"The police question him?"

"Yes."

"Is—that what you're worried about?"

"Partly. They brought several people to the station for questioning—even Carter Aubery and some people from out of town. Anyone they could find who was near the statue or Hank, or thought they were. The museum officials, of course. Even Howard's secretary. But they—the police—know Hank and Mike were arguing."

"But the statue's falling was an accident," said a surprised Dolly.

"No one is saying it isn't. Maybe that's what's worrying me so. You see, according to both Howard and Mike the casting was anchored to the pedestal by some kind of locking mechanism. Mike explained it to me sometime back, but I didn't pay attention to what he was saying at the time. It appears that the only way the statue could have toppled—"

"Someone would have had to unlock the mechanism?"

Lisa silently nodded yes.

"With that multitude of well-wishers, almost anyone of five hundred people could have unlocked it—and not maliciously, either. Curiosity, maybe."

Sitting on the edge of the bed, Dolly chimed in: "Charlie's right. Why, I looked at those statues and castings very carefully when I first arrived, and I remember thinking then that they were dangerous."

"It was a new way to display them. Mike's idea."

"Oh," said Charlie, catching the drift.

"Yes," said Lisa knowingly. "Mike's invention ... Mike and Ullman quarrelling ... Ullman dead."

"They—the papers—said he was sitting on a bench when the casting fell."

"I guess, Dolly. Hank could have been standing and the statue would have done its deed without difficulty. Dwarfish man. They called him Toulouse, you know."

"Who?" asked Charlie.

"People who didn't like him. I didn't like him myself, but I never called him Toulouse."

"Any idea what the argument was about?"

"Mike said it was museum business. Nothing more."

"I'm certain that's all it was," said Dolly, reaching over and patting her friend's knee.

Lisa bit her lip in concentration, rose and walked to the picture window.

"I'm not."

"What makes you say that?"

"Because, Charlie, I've—I've been waiting for something like this to happen. I've been here in Phoenix only three months, but from the very first day ... I've been frightened."

"Of *what*?"

"I wish I knew. Perhaps—perhaps it was the change in Mike. Yes, that must have been it. At least in the beginning."

"Can you explain that? The change?"

"I can try. May I have another cigarette?"

Charlie tossed her the pack and reached for matches.

"No, my hand is steady now."

She picked up a lighter from a low table and lit her cigarette, took a deep puff, and began slowly:

"About a year ago—when I first met Michael—things were wonderful. He had an easy way about him and he had class. I seem to overdo that word, don't I, Charlie? You caught me overdoing it yesterday."

"Go on."

"Somehow he met Gina Langley and her crazy mother."

"Crazy?"

"You'll meet her in time and you'll see what I mean. Not that she's any stranger than Gina. They're crazy in different ways. Gina liked him—Michael—and they hit it off. Gina's mother doted on Mike, too. They told him about their new museum—"

"Their museum?"

"I don't know all the legal technicalities, but somehow Gina got the city to let her have the land tax-free. I believe Carter Aubery contributed the building designs and the construction. Maybe there were a few others in on it, too. I—I don't know."

"I see."

"Just before I came out, Mike flew into New York. That's when I first noticed he'd changed. He seemed older. Nervous. Afraid."

"Did you speak to him about it?"

"No, I thought it was getting settled in a new place, that sort of thing. When I came out here I met them all—the board of directors at the museum. A close-knit group. To tell the truth, after I got to know them a bit I had half a mind to grab Mike by the hand and run for New York. Especially after what happened at Gina's."

"And what happened at Gina's?"

"I went out there one evening. Talk about a Waddington painting! Gina had just entered her Spanish mood."

She read their expressions.

"Odd, isn't it? Gina goes through phases. If she's feeling terribly Russian one year, she gets Russian servants, tricks up the house with samovars, calls herself Olga or some such thing."

Dolly was fascinated.

"They were all at Gina's. A board meeting, I guess. I rang the bell several times. No answer. Finally I began to pound on the door. No one responded, but their cars were all in the driveway. I tried the door. It was unlocked so I went in. I wish I hadn't."

"And were they there?"

"Yes. The lights were low. They were in the study. That room's like a cavern. Something out of the Middle Ages."

"You keep saying *they*. Who precisely?"

Lisa put her hand to her forehead, as if she were experiencing a headache.

"Let me think a moment ... Gina, naturally. She was seated ... Mike was there, Mrs. Crowley—that's Gina's mother ... Carter Aubery ... Some I didn't know ... Stacey ... Lars, too—I think, but I'm not positive."

"Did you announce yourself?"

"I didn't have time. Gina started to get up, then she started to sing and all the time she had this flower in her hand. Howard saw me, and signaled Mike and he came over, grabbed my arm and practically pulled me from the room."

"I see."

"It wasn't like Mike. He's worked very hard, Charlie, for everything he's ever gotten. And he's always been gentle and considerate. Now when it looks as if things might be heading somewhere for him, there's this mess with Hank."

"Did you ask him what was going on?"

"Yes. He got very angry. Said he had told me to wait outside at Gina's. Wait until he came out, but I didn't recall him saying that."

Charlie toyed with the button on his sports shirt.

"You said you were waiting for something to happen—"

"It's because of the people concerned with the museum. All so strange. Mike didn't get back from the police until early this morning. He feels the police suspect him. I know he does. Please help him, Charlie."

"So far, Lisa, there isn't any problem. You're insinuating, whether you realize it or not, that there was foul play with Ullman's death."

She hesitated before saying, "I—I guess I am. It's Mike I'm worried about, that's all. If it were only Ullman, perhaps, I wouldn't be so frantic, but Ullman and the phone calls—"

"What phone calls?"

"Mike's been getting them fairly regularly. I was at his apartment the first time he got one—at least I think it was the first time. The phone rang, Mike picked it up, and got very excited and kept repeating, 'Who is this, who is this? Jerry?' When he put down the receiver he was sweating. Literally."

"He didn't explain the call?"

"No—wouldn't discuss it. He pretended it was a wrong number."

"Have you any idea what the call might be?"

"I didn't then. I do now."

Charlie was very interested. "And—"

"Sometimes when I was there the phone would ring and he'd answer. He wouldn't say anything, so I knew what it was. This morning—right after he returned from police headquarters, it rang. He wouldn't pick it up. I asked him why he didn't and he told me to mind my own business."

Lisa began to sob quietly and Dolly came to her side.

"Poor kid, take it easy."

"You said," Charlie insisted, "you know what the call was. Or is."

Lisa wiped at her eyes with the back of her hand.

"It rang again, after Mike went into his bedroom and slammed the door. I lifted the receiver. So insane, I couldn't believe what he was saying. One sentence. One question, then he hung up. I was so confused I scribbled it down on a piece of paper to make certain I wasn't going as crazy as Gina."

Charlie's words took on a commanding tone. "What did the caller ask?"

Lisa pulled a slip of paper from her purse, clutched it for a moment before saying, "Please, Charlie, you've got to help Mike before something terrible happens to him."

"Let me see that piece of paper."

She handed it to him. Charlie unfolded it and read the words. He looked at Lisa, bewildered.

"What is it, Charlie? What does it say?" Dolly was anxious.

Outside by the pool, the woman in the leopard swimsuit trotted by on her way to a terrace breakfast.

"It's a question alright, Dolly."

"What did the caller ask?"

Charlie sat down on the bed.

"The caller asked—" He paused, reading the words. "The caller asked: 'Where is Snow White buried?'"

Chapter Three

"Where is Snow White buried?" Charlie kept repeating it to himself.

"Ah, that is the question," Dolly would interject from time to time.

They were driving to the town of Carefree, a considerable distance from Phoenix, and on the desert. It was early the next morning and Dolly wasn't fully awake.

"Weird, wouldn't you say, pet?"

"Oh, it's weird, Charlie. Come to think of it, Lisa was always getting into funny situations when I knew her in New York."

"How so?"

"One time she thought she was going to marry a man from Afghanistan."

"Not so funny."

"You'd think so if you saw him. Could slice cheese with his nose. He told her he was a prince. That kind of thing. Turned out they wanted him for bad checks in Mexico or some such rot. Wasn't a prince at all."

"What became of him?"

"What becomes of anyone in New York? After him it was some kook who wanted to open a cabaret in the village and push Zen."

"How do you push Zen?"

"His terminology, not mine. The point I'm making is that Lisa was always running around in circles. Believe me, when I saw her out here, I was surprised. She's matured. So much. I was delighted—now, she's back in a stew again."

"Wouldn't say this was her fault."

"You mean Ullman?"

"Like Lisa, I'm not sure I know what I mean."

"Shouldn't you have spoken to Mike Jarvits first? Before going to see Howard Stacey?"

"No, I don't think so. From everything Lisa's told me, the last thing he'd want snooping around is a private investigator. She doesn't want him to know. Might mean complications for her."

"Divorce cases are less complicated, aren't they, dear?"

"Indeed, they are."

"Nice of Howard Stacey to say he'd see us."

"Had hoped to see him at the museum, but it's closed on Tuesdays."

Dolly rested her head against the seat and shut her eyes. They had rented a white convertible and as it sped along the desert terrain, Dolly hummed, "Some Day My Prince Will Come."

Howard Stacey lived in a rundown barn/studio, not far from what passed as the Carefree town center: a gathering of a dozen shops catering to the winter tourist trade.

He met them at the door dressed in paint-stained dungarees and a grimy work shirt.

"Ah, the Underwoods. Mrs. Underwood, how charming you look this morning."

At Mountain Shadows, Dolly had purchased a squaw dress, a creation designed after a Navajo garment. Soft brown and white, it was trimmed with silver-metallic lacing. It suited her.

"Don't know if I'll be able to wear this in the East. Almost like a costume, isn't it?"

"Certainly not; that dress could be worn anywhere. To be sure, more important than the dress is the wearer."

Dolly relished the flattery. Howard ushered them in.

The barn was divided into two areas; the first was the main floor of the barn, which served as Howard's work studio. It went clear to the roof, broken by an occasional beam, while a loft apparently served as a bedroom. Done with taste and some imagination it could have been attractive. Charlie and Dolly had seen countless barns turned into homes of utmost charm. They had even discussed the possibility of doing it themselves in New Hampshire.

Howard Stacey's abode, however, looked like what it was. Exactly. Charlie could have sworn the aroma of cattle lingered. Howard seated them by his worktable.

"How about some coffee?"

"I'd adore a cup," said Dolly. "Charlie got me up so early, there wasn't time for any at the resort. And I kept thinking we'd pass a roadside café or something."

"Once you're on the desert," said Howard with a grin, "you're on the desert."

Dolly thought he was making a point she didn't catch, but she followed the wisdom of her deceased grandmother: "When you don't know what to say—smile!"

Dolly smiled.

"How about you, Charlie? Coffee?"

"Please."

A large tomato can, passing for a percolator, sat atop a single burner. Howard found some ceramic cups hidden behind a mound of paint cloths and pulled them out. They looked none too clean. Charlie and Dolly said nothing, being rather taken by the preparation.

Howard picked up a small plastic funnel and popped it into a cup, tilted the tomato can over this and allowed a stream of brownish liquid to stream forth.

"Cream? Sugar?"

"Both," said Dolly weakly.

Sugar was a single saccharin tablet with no apology. Cream was a tablespoon from a jar labeled "Substitute."

Dolly took her cup and sipped. She wished she hadn't. Charlie braved a few swallows.

"You—you have an interesting studio here, Howard," Dolly said.

"Home to me. It is. Basically, I'm an artist myself."

The Underwoods glanced around the studio. Few paintings were in evidence, and these were reproductions.

"Oh, no, no—not that kind of artist. I wouldn't presume. Here, *here* is my artistry."

He had been sitting on a high stool. He rose and went to a second table which was covered with a soiled white sheet, and threw it back with a flourish. Dolly came close to a gasp.

On the table were two dead squirrels, a hawk, an infant bobcat, and a menacing-looking creature, the likes of which Dolly have never before seen.

"Looks a mite grim at the moment, but when they're finished they'll look wonderful. Wonderful, I say."

"You're a taxidermist?"

"In my spare time."

Dolly stood and came close to the table.

"What is this thing? The one that's half-stuffed?"

Howard winced at her description.

"A Javelina, Dolly. Haven't you seen a Javelina?"

"I doubt it. I don't recall, anyway."

"Wild pig, isn't it?"

"Correct, Charlie. Wild pig—herds of them down around Tucson. They smell frightful, but the mother instinct of the Javelina is enviable."

Dolly looked at the pig's face: it was ugly, with sharp teeth jetting out in a dare. Dolly was prone to remark, "Mother instinct? I can imagine. Only a mother could love a face like that. *Ugh.*"

"You must come back and see her when she's finished."

"Oh, the Javelina's a she?"

"This one is."

Dolly squinted. Even when she distorted her features, Dolly had a mischievous beauty about her.

"Yes, I think you're right, Howard—a *she*. Looks something like a woman at the Shadows. Runs around in a leopard swimsuit."

Charlie said, "Ha, Ha."

"I see," beamed Howard, "something of a private joke."

"Dolly's having some fun, that's all."

Howard pulled the sheet over his array.

"Charlie, when you called this morning you said I could help you. Something about Hank's tragedy?"

"Yes."

"Don't know if I can be of any assistance that'll amount to anything. But go ahead."

"I'm curious about the pedestal."

"Ah, yes. And so were the police. Come here, I'll show you."

He led them to a corner of the barn where several pedestals, similar to those in the museum, stood like sentinels. He began to explain:

"The pedestals themselves are marble. Impossible to move. Or close to impossible. Go ahead, push a little."

Charlie stepped in and tried to budge the marble. He was able to move it slightly, no more.

"Try to topple it."

He tried. No success.

"See, the pedestal would not have fallen, even if great pressure one way or the other were applied."

Charlie concentrated on his thoughts before saying, "But the castings could be moved."

"Indeed so. Heavy. Take quite a push, but it could have been done, except all the castings were locked in position. Here, I'll show you."

He hoisted a plaster-of-Paris Buddha to the marble.

"This is a model. Light."

"I understand."

"Come in closer. You too, Dolly."

Howard moved Buddha to one side.

"Notice in the middle of the pedestal stand there's something of a depression?"

The Underwoods nodded.

"Put in your finger, Charles."

Charlie did as he was told.

"Notice anything unusual?"

"Around the edge of the depression—under—a thin ledge."

"Right."

Howard lifted the Buddha.

"Here on the bottom is a metal twist. Steel. What you do is to place the statue squarely over the depression." He did this. "Actually, the depression leaves space jetting out to the rear, and you slip your finger under and twist the steel bar, which then braces itself with a twist under the ledge. Impossible to budge it."

"Unless someone twists it back from the under-ledge position."

"I'm afraid so," Howard said sadly.

"No other way the bronze could have toppled?"

"None that I'm aware of."

"Odd that no one saw anyone do it."

"Oh, almost anyone could have unlatched the base."

"No, I mean about pushing the bronze. The marble wouldn't have budged. Whoever did it would have had to push directly at the casting."

"You're making it so rather deliberate."

"I suppose I am."

After a moment of silence—awkward silence—Howard said, "I think the detectives at the station have that same thought."

They returned to their chairs.

Charlie said, "Isn't that a rather unusual manner to place statuary? That steel holding latch."

"Couldn't agree with you more. Mike Jarvits invented it. Has a patent on it, though I doubt if any other museum but Gina's would utilize it. She has a terrible fear of things falling."

"Extraordinary women, Mrs. Crowley and her daughter."

"So I've been told. Howard, did you find out what young Jarvits and Ullman were arguing over?"

"Mike said it was over policy. Hank Ullman was on the board of directors. Mike wasn't. Hank was a—I hate to speak unkindly of the dead—"

"It may be important."

"I rather liked Hank—as much as any person *could* like him. He was very dictatorial in his manner. Something of a Fascist, I suppose. There was the wrong way to do something and the right way—*Hank's*. If you didn't want to do it his way, you were wrong and consequently—guilty."

"*Guilty?*"

"That was always Hank's way of looking at things. But to answer your question about Mike: Seems Hank told the staff not to hang any Remingtons."

"An artist?" Dolly asked.

"Frederick Remington. One of the finest old masters of western art. Three paintings were donated and we—the staff, Mike included—were delighted, but Hank was not. You see, he felt western art, the cowboy and Indian, if you will, did not constitute art at all. Likened it to a calendar display. And he was adamant on the topic. He gave orders that the paintings were not to be put up for the opening, but he spoke for himself, not the board. Mike knew this and went right ahead and hung them."

"Judging from Ullman's manner, he *was* infuriated."

"Well, he's not going to be infuriated anymore."

The Underwoods were startled. So was Howard.

"Oh, I beg your pardon. That was a dreadful thing to say. I assure you I didn't mean it to sound that way."

"We understand," added Dolly with empathy.

"The board," pondered Charlie aloud, "*who* precisely is on the board?"

"Easy enough," brightened Howard. "Myself, Gina (always Gina), her mother, Mrs. Crowley—"

"She's the one who's—" Dolly caught herself in mid-sentence.

"Then you've met her?"

"No, no. But Lisa mentioned her, I believe."

"You must see their house. Have Mike take you there. Gina was in a Spanish phase. Spanish Colonial. But I understand that's changing. No telling what you'll see."

"The board," requested Charlie flatly.

"Yes, the board. Gina and her mother. Hank. Not anymore, of course. And Carter Aubery. Dorothea was, but she left town some months ago."

"Dorothea?"

"Dorothea Darnell—a protégé of Gina's. Only five on the board now."

"Four," corrected Dolly.

Howard paled. "That's true. Will you be attending the funeral? No, naturally you wouldn't be. Loathe the things myself. This won't be too hard to take, however. Memorial service. At the museum. Cremated, you know. I understand Gina wants the remains in a niche in the Shelly room. She calls it that. Actually, it's all pre-Raphael paintings. Remington's more my speed."

Charlie got up from the comfort of a worn armchair. Dolly followed suit.

"Leaving so soon? Wouldn't you care for another cup?"

"No, no, thank you," Dolly insisted.

"Nothing else I can tell you, then?"

Charlie felt in his coat pocket. The note Lisa had scribbled was there.

"Out of curiosity—and I know this sounds peculiar—but apart from the fairy tale, does the name 'Snow White' mean anything to you, Howard?"

"Certainly."

Charlie was stunned, but managed, "What?"

"That's what everyone called Dorothea—'Snow White'—skin as white as snow; hair black as ebony. That was our Dorothea. Strikingly handsome girl."

"You wouldn't know where she's living now?"

"No, but I'm quite sure Gina would. Gina knows everything. If you're going out there, do me a favor."

"Surely," answered Dolly.

He went to the sheet-covered table and pulled a stuffed Gila monster and handed it to a most uncomfortable Mrs. Underwood.

"Give her this for me. Tell her I love her."

Neither Charlie nor his wife said a word until they reached the car.

Then they couldn't say enough.

Chapter Four

Breakfast was served on a terrace high above the swimming pool compound. The hour was shortly before nine and many of the cabanas still had drapes drawn across their windows as protection against the morning sun.

Only a few of the tables were occupied and—from what Dolly could see—grapefruit and black coffee was the favored meal.

"Never could get by with just that. Not me. Why am I always famished in the morning? Why is that, Charlie—*me* being famished?"

His mouth was open, unintentionally, and his eyes followed the dramatic creature as she regally ascended the steps to the terrace. Her hair was raven black, her natural grace in movement rather provocative.

"Shut your mouth," suggested Dolly, although not belligerently.

The woman sat, ramrod straight, at a table nearby. The Filipino waiter brought the breakfast menu and poured some ice water from a large crystal pitcher.

"The Leopard Woman," hissed Dolly.

The fascinator smiled pleasantly at Charlie, winked, and turned her attention to the menu.

"Are you awake or sleepy?"

"Huh?"

"Would you like me to introduce you, Charlie?"

Without thinking, he said breathily, "Do you know her name?"

"Leopard Woman." Her expression was impish.

Charlie snapped out of his hypnotic state quickly, "Sorry, baby. She's—"

"No need to explain, pet. Eat your jam like a good little boy."

He looked at his wife with amusement etched on his tanned face.

"I was saying I couldn't get by on just coffee in the morning. Remember those marvelous breakfasts in Norway? Great slabs of cheese, eggs, pastry. I love to eat. Yet, I never seem to gain weight. I'm as slim as when you married me. Right?"

"*Right!*"

"Not necessary to say it with quite so much conviction. More coffee?"

He held out his cup.

"This is an improvement on what we had yesterday at this time."

"You mean at Howard Stacey's?"

"Yeah." He took a swallow of coffee.

"Strange man, I think. I mean—to head that museum. The museum's chichi and he impresses me as—uh—"

"Something of a hayseed?"

"At least."

He glanced at the Leopard Woman. She was nodding at something the waiter was saying.

"He told us about Snow White."

"What do you make of that?"

"At the moment—nothing. What's interesting is the last word of the phone call."

Dolly picked up a piece of crisp bacon and popped it into her mouth.

"*Buried?*"

"Yes, Dolly. *Buried.*"

He put down his cup and wiped his mouth on a yellow cloth napkin.

"Of course, we're not safe in assuming that Snow White and this Dorothea are one and the same." Then, she added cautiously, "Are we?"

"I'd assume they were one and the same, bright one."

She found "bright one" more irritating than rebuttal.

"Oh."

"Think it out for yourself. Everyone called this Miss Darnell 'Snow White.' According to Howard, Snow White left town sometime ago. A mysterious phone call plaguing one Mike Jarvits asks where Snow White is buried."

"But, Charlie—that would mean she's dead."

He gave his wife a cool appraising glance. "For her sake, I hope so."

Dolly made a throaty sound.

"What's on the docket for today?"

Charlie stretched back and relaxed, his head braced against his folded hands.

"I've called down to the station."

"Police station?"

"No, dear, the fire station," he said in a grumble. "I've called down to the *police* station and talked to a detective in charge of the Ullman investigation. I'll drop you off at Lisa's. Get her out to Gina's and make an appointment. Also, pump her for information on this Dorothea gal. Lisa may know something."

Dolly gingerly lifted Charlie's uneaten toast from his plate.

"You still hungry?"

"Got to keep up my strength to fight off the leopards."

Police headquarters was in an ugly, oblong building in the downtown section of Phoenix, surrounded by pawn shops, chili parlors and flop houses.

The detective that greeted Charlie was a lean man with silver-gray hair, very distinguished and rather handsome.

"A pleasure," he said, warmly shaking Charlie's hand. Read about your exploits with that war criminal. Switzerland, wasn't it?"

"Liechtenstein."

"Right you are."

The detective, Tod Van Spanckeren, indicated a chair, and Charlie sat.

"What is it precisely that I can do to help you?"

Charlie smiled. "The word *precisely* throws me."

"I know what you mean. About Ullman, huh?" He sat behind his desk and reached for a brown folder.

Charlie said, "Come up with anything?"

"That's one of the problems. I'm not convinced it is possible to come up with anything. A mob of people were pushing around that pedestal. Ullman standing wasn't much taller than Rumpelstiltskin—when the bronze hit, he was sitting down and it did the trick good."

"Anyone going to be booked?"

"On what? For what? We must have questioned two dozen people. No one saw it fall, happened that quick. He didn't even yell out. Didn't slide to the floor, either—at first. Place was too crowded for that."

Charlie took out a pack of cigarettes, offering one to Van Spanckeren, who declined.

"Go ahead. They're Egyptian. Ever had an Egyptian cigarette?"

"No, but I'll try anything once."

He accepted a light from Charlie, who leaned across the desk.

"What about Mike Jarvits?"

"Ah, on the track, I see." He laughed good-naturedly.

"Curious."

"Nothing there. Sure, they had an argument and many people saw them arguing, but you can't prove anything by that. Besides, Henry Ullman was a man who had many enemies."

"Oh?"

"Many of his enemies were at that opening. But that doesn't mean they engineered that weird bopping."

Charlie flicked cigarette ash in a tray modeled in the shape of the State's outline.

"So how do things stand at present?"

"Looks to me like accidental death. If it wasn't I don't know how the hell we're going to be able to prove anything. They're a ticklish bunch, too. As much trouble from that angle as any other."

"Who do you mean?"

Van Spanckeren rose and walked a few steps to the window. His office was on the fourth floor and, as he spoke, he took unconscious note of the comings and goings on the street below.

"Let me put it to you this way. This town's growing like hell is supposed to—according to revivalists who flood in here every winter, that is. They never seem to come in the summer. Too damn hot. Growing. But at the same time, this is a small town. A few people control most of what goes on. Perhaps the papers, the banking, the cultural life— "

"I'm beginning to get the picture."

"So when they're embarrassed in any way—mind you, I'm not suggesting anything—but let's say when a woman as wealthy and influential as Gina Langley opens a million-dollar museum, she wants nice publicity. Understand?"

"I'm beginning to."

"I'm saying this for your sake as much as mine—should you be planning on stirring up anything. You're not, are you?"

"Not planning to," Charlie said, thinking.

"Then no one's hired you about this Ullman death?"

"I haven't been hired by anyone, no."

"Good. Because there's nothing to go on."

Charlie sighed. "It's beginning to look that way. I wonder if I could check out something with your Missing Persons Bureau?"

"Anything you want. Who're you looking for?"

"A gal named Dorothea Darnell."

"Who's she?"

"Now it's your turn to ask the questions, huh?"

Over Charlie's protests, Van Spanckeren made several inter-office phone calls. None brought forth any information regarding the whereabouts of Miss Darnell. She had not been reported missing, nor did her name appear in the city registry.

"Dead end," said the detective. "Can you give me anything else to go on?"

Charlie was annoyed, but concealed his mood with "Afraid not, but thanks for the trouble."

"No trouble at all," the detective said smilingly. "Keep in touch, and if you do stumble across anything—anything at all—do let me know."

Charlie got up, stamping out his cigarette as he did so.

"You sound as if you half expect me to find something."

The detective's vocal moods were subtly changeable. Almost apologetically, he said, "That's one of our weaknesses here. The department. We're always there after something has happened. We rarely stumble onto something, but then, that's one way to make certain we don't stumble at all." Charlie didn't understand, but made no comment.

The policeman shook hands. The New Englander was confused. Van Spanckeren hadn't been of any help; more than this, he seemed to be teasing, subtly defiant, and Charlie had no way of counter-attacking.

He was halfway down the corridor when the detective called out to him. Charlie turned. Van Spanckeren was in the doorway to his office. He was holding his nose, brandishing what remained of the Egyptian cigarette.

"What do they make these things out of? Mummy wrappings?"

His cultivated smoothness had been temporarily shattered.

Ah, thought Mr. Underwood to himself, the pleasure of retaliation.

Lisa lived in a housing development called Pancho Villa's Villa. The dwelling, incredibly tiny, as if doll people were the likely tenants, were arranged in jumbled streets, some stuck on artificial hills to add to the hoped-for effect of a Mexican seacoast village. There were about 300 casitas in the pseudo-township, and Dolly knew only that Lisa lived at number 126.

No easy matter to locate the place, for all designations were made in Spanish—e.g. *Numero Uno*—and Dolly knew no Spanish. Even if she had, finding the place would have remained something of a challenge, for the numbering was not consecutive.

After fifteen minutes of frantic searching she found number 126, thanks to the services of a young boy who found her charming and had asked in all sincerity if Dolly would care to be his mother.

She rapped at the door and a moment later it was opened by a very wan and tired ex-hoofer.

"Come in, Dolly."

"You look like death."

"Feel like it, too."

Lisa went to put some coffee on, despite her friend's attempts to dissuade her. Dolly sat in a chair much too small for human occupancy.

"How long have you lived in this place, Lisa?"

"Ever since I came to Phoenix. Why?"

"No special reason. Reminds me of Disneyland or something like that."

Lisa came from the kitchen, which was nothing more than an indented wall section, cut off from the main room.

"I didn't have much money, and I wasn't going to have Mike support me until after we were married, so it was this place. Rent's cheap. It was this place or Old Virginia City—that's the development across the street. I thought Pancho Villa's Villa was more southwestern, you know?"

"Yes, I know."

Lisa excused herself and changed into a light blue dress. (She'd been wearing a drab chenille robe when Dolly arrived.) Dolly decided she would have some coffee after all and poured two cups. When Lisa reappeared from the midget bedroom, she appeared somewhat chipper.

"Did you see Mike last night?"

"Yes, I did," she replied, sitting in a chair opposite Dolly.

"And?"

The chipperness faded: "He's not Mike. That's all I can say. We went out for dinner. He wanted to. But he didn't touch a mouthful. He barely talked."

Lisa was possessed of a tremendous sadness and Dolly's sympathy went out to her old friend.

"I thought this was it—the pot of gold at the end of the rainbow. Me and Mike. Now—now, I don't know."

Reassuringly, Dolly offered: "Chin up. The show must go on."

Lisa forced a kind of smile and took a sip of her coffee.

"Has Charlie found out anything yet?"

"Not yet, dear. It'll take time. Charles is a wonderful detective. I don't say that merely because I'm his wife, but because it's true. He wants you to call Mrs. Langley and make an appointment for us."

"Gina?"

"Yes."

"But, what good will that do?"

"Charlie thinks it's important."

"All right, but she's not easy to talk to—unless—"

"*Unless?*"

"Unless she wants to be. She likes young men, so maybe Charlie's in luck."

Dolly frowned. The Leopard was quite enough.

"I'll call now."

Dolly interrupted: "Lisa, we went out to Howard Stacey's yesterday."

"In Carefree?"

"Yes, in that smelly stable."

Lisa rose and nervously began to pace.

"What did Charlie find out?"

Dolly was losing patience.

"Nothing. What could he find out? For goodness sake, Lisa, get control of yourself."

Dolly smiled pleasantly, hoping to put her friend at ease.

"Lisa, did you ever hear of a woman named Darnell? Dorothea Darnell?"

When this question was asked, Lisa had her back to Dolly. On hearing the words she spun around and spat rather accusingly, "Why—why do you ask about her?"

The questioner was stunned by the rudeness. Dolly met the challenge: "Because her name came up in the course of discussion and Charlie felt it might be important. Important to you and Mike."

"I've never heard of her."

Lisa was a frightful liar and she, herself, realized how badly she performed. She paused, went to the window and opened the drapes, staring out across the plaza where cement Mexican soldiers stood guard.

Slowly, she began: "I think she might have been the girl who worked for Gina."

"In what capacity?"

"Secretary or something. With Gina you never know. She has people in and out of her employ constantly. Yes, I think I do recall the name. That's the girl, yes."

Lisa kept her eyes glued to the cement men. Some time passed before Dolly asked, "Why were you so swift in denying that you knew her?"

"No—no reason. I think I would have bitten at any question you asked. I didn't sleep well last night. Not a wink."

"Then you shouldn't be drinking that coffee. Why don't you put in that call to Gina Langley?"

The suggestion seemed to relieve Lisa and she gushed, "Yes, yes, I'll do that now. Hope we don't get Mrs. Crowley on the phone. Every time it rings she races the servants for it."

She dialed and waited.

"Hello, hello. Juan?"

"Juan, this is Miss Lynch. Lisa Lynch ... fine, thank you ... Is Mrs. Langley at home? Hello, *hello*?"

Lisa put her hand over the mouthpiece and said to Dolly, "Mrs. Crowley is fighting for the phone. I knew it ... Hello, Juan, *hello*? Oh, it's you, Mrs. Crowley . . . Lynch . . . Lisa Lynch. We've met several times." She made a sour expression. "Yes, Mrs. Crowley," she boomed defensively, "I'm the girl who dances. Is your daughter at home? . . . *daughter*? Gina! Gina, Mrs. Crowley, Gina! . . . She's down at the kennels? With the dogs, yes. I see ... Would you be kind enough to have her call me when ... Hello, hello? . . . Juan, is that you? . . . Yes, I understand, Juan. Thank you ever so much."

She hung up.

"Lord," she said with a deep breath, "calling that place is like calling Bedlam. Juan says he'll have her call me back."

"Mrs. Crowley?"

"Gina. No, Mrs. Crowley doesn't call out."

"You make her sound like a prisoner."

"You'll understand when you meet her. She has a mind like a dusty room."

Abruptly, Lisa moved from the telephone and dashed to a small table, snatching a pack of cigarettes in one impulsive gesture. Dolly watched as Lisa attempted to light the tobacco, but her hand shook so, that both the cigarette and match fell to the floor. The flame quickly died, and Lisa collapsed on a seat-and-a-half sofa, a specialty of the Villa's furnishing cubicles.

Dolly came to her.

"Don't you worry, baby. Your friends are here. There's nothing to fret about. Charles will solve everything. He'll get to the bottom of this. You'll have your wedding and live happily ever after."

Dolly Underwood listened to herself prattle nonsense and rather enjoyed it.

They were back at Mountain Shadows about the time of sunset, a spectacularly beautiful part of the Arizona evening. Vistas of desert beauty reached in all directions, coloring the landscapes with crimson hues that spanned the spectrum from black and deep purple to a flaming orange. Dolly had never seen anything like it.

They were discussing the view as they entered the main lobby and encountered Mike Jarvits.

He was attired meticulously; his tie knotted a bit too tight, so that a thick line of rawness protruded above his starched collar.

"I've got to talk to you."

"Let's go down to the cabana. Easier to talk there."

"What I have to tell you won't take long."

Charlie looked at him closely. The sparkle in his eyes was too bright; he was close to being tight, but held his liquor like a gentleman. One or two more, however ...

"I know Lisa's been after you to find out it if I killed Hank Ullman." This took Charlie aback.

"That's foolish. Who've you been talking to?"

"Never mind."

"Did Howard Stacey tell you?"

"There's nothing here for you, Charlie. Lisa's upset because I haven't been myself lately. A personal problem. Forget it. Enjoy your holiday in the sun and then head back to New Hampshire."

"You make that sound like a threat."

"No threat. But I want you off my tail. You let me manage Lisa."

There was no sense arguing with the man.

"Okay," said Charlie rather cheerfully. "Any way you want it."

Mike faced them awkwardly, not knowing what his next move should be. He mumbled, "Lisa is an excitable kid. I—I don't like to be investigated, that's all."

He was about to say something else when he changed his mind and headed for the bar, a few steps away.

They watched him enter. The end stool was occupied by the Leopard Woman, still alone, still friendly.

She gave Charlie a smile and held up her glass in salute.

By the time the Underwoods reached their cabana, the sunset had deepened into night.

Day was dead.

Chapter Five

"Why are mounts of red rock usually referred as cathedrals?"

From under the newspaper covering Charlie's face came a muf-fled, "Ermph."

"What?"

He made the sound again. This time it sounded like nothing at all. Dolly grabbed for the paper. They had spent the morning sunbath-ing by the pool and, although the sun was not overly powerful, it cast an exceedingly strong glare. Dolly wore a one-piece swimsuit, pinkish in color, and from a distance one got the distinct impression she was nude. This, she discovered, by the clustering of Filipino wait-ers who wiped the tables by the terrace rail over and over again.

When they returned to their room after the encounter with Mike Jarvits the previous evening, there was a phone message waiting. Gina Langley had called and she would be able to see the Under-woods the following afternoon.

Newspaper off his face, Charlie winced in the sunlight.

"Hey, I was sleeping."

"And I was asking you a question."

"What question?"

"In travel books and things, why do writers describe bunches of red rocks as cathedrals?"

He looked at her sourly, but said gently, "I don't know." He was more than slightly annoyed.

Charlie yawned and glanced at the magazine she was reading: *Arizona Highways*. He had finished with his reading, which was a rundown on Mrs. Langley by a local society writer.

"Not much here," he said stifling the desire to yawn again, "that we didn't know already, I'm afraid."

Dolly sat with her knees tucked under her chin.

"Does it give her age?"

He reached down and picked the book from atop a bunched blue towel. "No, but she can't be any younger than sixty. She was a movie queen in the silent era, remember?"

She looked at her husband coquettishly. "I don't remember. And I shouldn't think you would."

"I remember the name certainly. Gloria Swanson, Marion Davies, Gina La Rue."

Dolly noted the interest of the waiters before continuing on with the conversation. "You make them sound like The Three Stooges."

"Seems she kept the La Rue part for a while, even after her marriage to Langley. Gina La Rue Langley; then simply–Gina Langley. According to this rundown, Mr. Langley's family owned everything in this town worth owning at one time or other. Family had two governors, three congressmen, a senator. Real First Family of Arizona stuff. Says Gina was married to some Rumanian director in the mid-twenties, gives a list of her stage plays and films, some books I never heard of that she authored. Coupled with hubby's fortune, I'd say Mrs. Langley was quite something."

"*Is*, Charlie. She's still alive, you know. I'm glad she called. I'm very anxious to see the place."

"You mean to see what *phase* she's in? I wonder why she called us personally, instead of having Lisa do it."

Dolly stretched out supine. "When I saw Lisa yesterday at that— Pancho's Villa, or whatever it's called—"

"Pancho Villa's Villa."

"When I saw her there she was terribly upset, but I told her you'd get to the bottom of the phone calls, and once you discovered what they were all about, things would work themselves out."

He stood, lifting his arms high over his head.

"Simple as ABC, huh? She got hot under the collar when you mentioned Dorothea, you say?"

"More than that. She exploded, denying she knew the name at first."

"Wonder why?"

"So do I, but she calmed down in almost no time. I think she knows considerably more about Dorothea than she's letting on."

Charlie began to do a series of stretching exercises.

"That's helpful, isn't it? She gets us into this mess and now starts to clam shut. That Tod Van Spanckeren at Police Headquarters wasn't exactly a bundle of information, either. Telling me in a nice polite way, real smooth, that it would be sugary for everyone concerned if I didn't step on any toes."

Dolly turned a page of her magazine.

"Who tipped off Mike?"

"Good question, but I don't know. Might have been Howard. Or Lisa in a fit of confession, maybe even our good friend, the gentleman at Police Headquarters. What is it they say out here–*Quién sabe?*"

"Beats me."

"Hey—"

"What?" She watched him catch sight of the waiters.

"Oh, *them*. Don't worry, darling. They think I'm nude, but I'm not. I'm no Leopard Woman, but I do alright."

She felt a whack to her rump from a towel Charlie was holding in his hand.

Gina Langley lived in an enormous rambling structure of adobe and grill work, halfway between Phoenix and the city of Scottsdale. Impossible to see the house from the road, being, as it was, hidden behind lush growths of oleanders and privet. There was a high gate at the entrance, but this was open and wide as they approached and drove straight through.

About an eighth of a mile up the dusty road they came to the house.

"I'm disappointed," said Dolly.

"Looks like quite a castle to me," countered Charlie.

"I guess I expected something more like, you know—that picture with Swanson—what was it?"

"Boulevard – *Sunset Boulevard!*"

"I expected something like that."

Charlie turned off the ignition.

"This is Arizona, baby, not Southern California."

"There's a difference?"

They got out and looked around. The house was surrounded by an orange grove and the trees gave off a hint of fragrance. The sky was clear and blue. This contemplative atmosphere was suddenly ripped by a shriek: *Kar–uuu!*

Dolly stepped close to her husband.

"What was that? Gina or Mrs. Crowley?"

The sound came a second time: *Kar–uuu!*

Strutting out to greet them was a gorgeous peacock, confident and impossibly regal.

Dolly laughed. "I guess I was mistaken. This place *is* beginning to live up to expectation."

They walked along a covered outer-hall until they reached what they assumed was the front door. Charlie rang.

The door was opened by a squat Mexican butler, out of breath and panting.

"Yes?" he inquired rather impatiently.

"Mr. and Mrs. Underwood."

"Yes?"

Dolly and Charlie exchanged a questioning look.

Dolly said, "We're expected."

It was the butler's turn to look puzzled. He stood in the doorway as if he wasn't certain what his course of action should be.

Dolly took charge. "Please tell Mrs. Langley that Mr. and Mrs. Underwood have arrived. As expected."

This got through to him and he smiled. Nearly. He stepped into the hallway and walked ahead, indicating that they should follow, which they did, bewildered but curious.

The butler led them to a small patio-garden and here they were told to wait. Charlie sat and lit a cigarette while his wife wandered around. The spot was enclosed on all sides by walls of the house, the patio thus forming something of an inner-courtyard. The gardening was cultivated and groomed, but in such a way that the place had nothing of a rigid or cold formality about it.

There were two very large aviaries. One empty, the other hosted two cockatoos, white and vain, and two macaws, noisy and quarrelsome. In nooks and crannies fine authentic statue representations of saints looked out serenely. Dolly would not have been surprised to see literature's Ramona wander from the house, her dark eyes sad, her gait lovely, her sorrow obvious. Instead, what popped out was an energetic and bizarre creature, weighted down with enough junk jewelry to open a wayside stand, looking too much like an eccentric to be one.

"Howdy-doo, howdy-doo!"

The woman was elderly, but indecently spry. She wore a wide-brimmed hat, straw, bonnet-styled, and it shaded most of her face. What was exposed was dusted heavily with rice powder. An orange Mandarin jacket, purple silk trousers, and gold-trimmed slippers completed the ensemble.

She hurried toward Dolly.

"Howdy-doo, howdy-doo."

Obviously the woman was Gina's mother, Mrs. Crowley.

She threw up her hands in surprise.

"But you're not wearing anything Oriental."

Dolly replied, calmly, "Was I supposed to?"

"Why, yes," answered the woman, somewhat put out. "The Spanish Colonial phase is over. Finished. Kaput. From now on everything's coming up Chinatown."

Charlie rose. "You're Mrs. Crowley?"

"That's a safe bet. You're occidental, too."

"I'm sorry," said Charlie, going along for the ride. "I didn't know we had entered a new—er—phase, either."

Mrs. Crowley turned her attention to the aviaries. "They'll have to go. And those saints—there."

Rapidly gesturing with a bony finger, she pointed from one statue to another. "To the museum. Whenever my girl is through with something it goes to the museum. That's what she built that thing for—don't tell her I told you—that's what she built it for—to unload her stuff. Girl bores easily. Why are we out here? Why aren't we inside for tea? I want my tea."

The butler returned to the patio and announced with no embarrassment. "You are not expected."

He stood to one side and with a wave of an open-palmed hand indicated the way out.

Mrs. Crowley saved the situation.

"They are too expected. Now go back and tell my daughter I invited them. I invited them, I say, and I say they stay. And tell cook to hustle with some tea things."

This turn of events didn't please him. Plainly he wanted to make a retort to the old woman, but the presence of the Underwoods deterred him. He made an attempt to restate his mistress' remark, but Mrs. Crowley silenced him with, "Move it!"

From the garden, very quickly, he moved.

"That was one of the things that was supposed to change," insisted Mrs. Crowley. "In the Orient servants are supposed to be cooperative and good. That fellow is not cooperative—and he's no damned good. Thinks I'm some kind of a nut. Not so. Gina's the kook. She ought to be in this cage, not these beautiful birds. Wonderful looking things, aren't they? Can't send them off to the museum. Wonder what Gina's planning for these feathered babies?"

Charlie shifted his weight nervously. "Excuse me, Mrs. Crowley, but *you* called yesterday at the Shadows and left the message?"

"Didn't I go through telling you all that? I? 'Course I did!"

"How did you know where we were staying?"

"I called that girl who dances—"

"Lisa Lynch?"

"*Does* she dance?"

"Not anymore," said Dolly.

"But she *did* once, didn't she?"

"Yes."

"Then it's probably the same one. I called her and asked where you were staying."

"But," Charlie began hesitantly, "the name left was Gina Langley."

"Don't think I'm demented enough to leave my own name, do you? If I did that you wouldn't have come. Only way I get any company is to call up people and tell them I'm Gina. They come running then, kids. Damn if they don't. But seal your lip with Gina."

Dolly nodded assent without knowing why, then she turned hopelessly to Charlie, who didn't look too happy about the whole thing himself.

The out-of-breath butler returned.

"She, Mrs. Langley, says, in that case to pretend you *are* expected."

"Here we go," exclaimed Mrs. Crowley, taking them by the arm and stepping out with a jaunty stride. "I knew she'd come along. Besides, she's bored again. That's always a good sign. Anything goes when my baby is bored. Oughta make a song out of that. I'm going to think about that very thing, I am."

Feeling like damn fools, the Underwoods had no choice but to go along with the unusual Mrs. Crowley.

The interior of the house was something of a rabbit warren. Corridors and sub-corridors wandered in and out, and most surprising was the fact that the house had a cellar or lower floor, a rarity in architectural design for any desert state. They saw three separate flights of stairs traveling downward. The change in "phase" was pronounced. More *Santos*, wooden this time, were pointed out by Mrs. Crowley, as they stood beside wooden crates marked "Memorial Museum."

The vestments of aged churchmen serving South and Central America were piled neatly on the top of magnificent wooden chests of carved mahogany. Chandeliers were strewn here and there as if they had crashed to the floor, only to be abandoned.

Contrasting with this scene were the curious art objects that would shortly take over the decoration chore. Dolly noted half a dozen servants scurrying in and out, some dressed as Mexican serving girls, others in dungarees and T-shirts, one in a long silk robe embroidered with a village scene on the back. Everything was in transition.

The butler, or the man the Underwoods assumed was the butler, stopped in front of a set of double doors and knocked. The voice that came in reply was gentle and inviting.

Dolly felt more at ease.

The man opened the doors, stepped to one side and ushered the trio in with a wave of his hand. Once inside the room, he closed the doors and was heard giving directions to the servants in the corridor.

The room was, indeed, as Lisa Lynch had described it: Cavernous. Yet, it was spared the commotion and unrest that seized the other parts of the house periodically. The room had more than a touch of permanency about it and the walls were covered with an art collection that stunned both Charlie and Dolly.

Charlie's knowledge of the art world was not inconsiderable, and through his recent adventure in Europe, he had learned even more about what was rapidly becoming something of an avocation. He recognized a Matisse and stopped on the spot. Reproductions of the painting he had seen many times before, but the painting on the wall nearest the door was no copy. The painting was almost eight feet high and well over twelve feet in length—it was practically a mural. The subject matter was five female nudes playing against a field of green and blue. He found it breathtaking.

"That is called," came Gina's voice from somewhere in the room, "*Dance*. It was done as a study for a mural commissioned by Sergei I. Schukin. Why are most Russians I know, red and white, named Sergei? Can you tell me that?"

They looked for her among the sofas and high-backed chairs.

"The one next to it is an Utrillo and the one next to that, as well." The Utrillo section was startling. He had never seen so many in one space.

"Come over here and meet me. My collection will be here long after I depart."

"She means the earth," snickered Mrs. Crowley.

Following the sound of her voice, they walked down the length of the room. Now and again, Charlie had no choice but to stop a moment and look at a painting. He picked out a Modigliani, a Manet, two he felt safe in assuming were by Orozco, and one that could have been a Picasso.

When at last they reached the end of the room it was obvious why they hadn't seen Gina right off. A high-back lounge faced a window fronting a second enclosed patio. A herd of odd canines sunned themselves here. Gina had been watching them.

"Come around where I can see you."

Mrs. Crowley held back, but Charlie and Dolly presented themselves before the famed celebrity.

She was, for her age, a remarkable female. Sunlight streamed through her windows giving her less of a break than she deserved, placing her under a merciless evaluator where every wrinkle and sag was in evidence. Still, even with this, Gina Langley was no slouch. Her face had a tight quality to it, and Dolly quickly thought to herself that surgery once or twice had been brought into play. Gina's auburn hair was soft and fluffy and framed her face perfectly in a casual manner. She wore a light lipstick and if she wore more cosmetics that this it was not easy to tell. A thin Chinese Mandarin costume, similar to the one worn by Mrs. Crowley, dressed her trim body. On Mrs. Crowley it was ludicrous, on Gina it worked. She was resting on the lounge and did not rise. Instead, in a Bronte tradition, she held up one hand, not too energetically, and Charlie shook it.

"Sit down," said Gina and she indicated two wide ottomans.

"Thank you for seeing us, Mrs.—"

"Are we alone, or is there someone with you?"

Mrs. Crowley was incensed.

"I'm here, Gina. You know I am. I am, too, here."

"Oh," said Gina almost sadly, "you've found mother."

"*They* didn't find *me*," said Mrs. Crowley defensively, and it was a shrill complaint. "*I* found *them*."

"Be quiet, Mother."

"We came at a bad time," Dolly said.

"One time is as good as any other. Haven't you read my book on the relation of time and space?"

"I don't recall," replied Charlie. "What was the title?"

Mrs. Crowley barked, "*Now and Never*. And nobody's read it. Last royalty check was for thirty dollars and seven cents."

Gina took no notice of her mother's words.

"In my book I bring out the theory that everything is not only relative but unimportant. If you have arrived at an awkward time, then mentally you must take the attitude that the hour could not be more auspicious."

"I must get a copy," said Dolly.

"Please do. I'd give you a copy, but I feel people rarely appreciate anything they receive for free."

"What she has to count pennies for is news to me."

Again, the daughter ignored the mother.

"You're the friends of Michael Jarvit's fiancée?"

"Yes," Charlie said.

"What do you think of Mr. Jarvits?"

"I haven't known him for long—just a few days. I've seen him a few times ... At the opening--"

"Ah, yes," said Gina wistfully, "the opening. Will you have a drink?"

"None for me," said Charlie. Dolly also declined.

"I'll take some sherry." Gina pointed to a decanter on a low table by Charlie. Three exquisite glasses were set on an Arabic tray. He poured her a glass and handed it to her.

"What do you think of my museum?"

"Remarkable. For a town this size. I mean, a private museum of its scope."

"Oh, the city has its finger in it, too. But basically it's mine. My doing. It troubles me to see so many people with art treasures doing nothing with them. Nothing at all. Not even looking at them. That's one reason I decided to open the museum. So when one is bored with a painting, a statue or a sculpture, one may donate it to my museum. There it will be lovingly displayed."

"This room is practically a museum in itself."

"Yes," said Gina in appreciation. "It is. I adore this room. Do most of my thinking here. It's like a church to me. Sanctuary. Every evening before I retire I come here, in front of these French doors and sip hot chocolate. I wonder why? Hot chocolate is such a peculiar drink at that time of night. Chocolate is heavy. One would think it would tend to keep one awake, but it doesn't me. Helps me sleep. Yes, every night I am here. Ritual. But, then, ritual belongs in a church."

She gestured to take in the room.

"Now, about Mr. Jarvits: your impression?"

"I really don't have one," replied Charlie.

"I'm sorry to hear that. I was impressed with him when I first encountered him. New York. Alive, peppery, with excellent ideas on what a progressive museum should be. A *privately* owned museum.

I have little in common with the rank and file. Instinctively, I'm an aristocrat."

Mrs. Crowley guffawed.

"Couldn't get the city's cooperation without having to take some of their dead weight, like Howard Stacey and his staff. Howard's family was very prominent here at one time. Pioneer stock. Beaver trappers originally, I believe. Stacey name means a great deal in Arizona and Howard knows it, but it's unfair, I think, to take advantage of a family name. My late husband's family had a much better name than that of Stacey, but I chose to make my own way. I lend a vitality to an old name. Howard lends nothing. That was the agreement. The city wouldn't close its museum—frightful place with old army rifles—and give me the land, even though I was going to finance everything, without that condition. Naturally, I had to bring in someone that had something. That's why I selected Michael. A mite short, and that Prussian hairstyle doesn't help, but he has a certain charm."

Charlie said, "He invented that steel twist for the statuary, didn't he?"

"Indeed he did. Every museum in the country is screaming about what I've done. They mean altering the base of any statue. I pay them no attention. Things falling distress me. An atavistic return, probably. Have you read *Flight?*"

Charlie shook his head.

"*Flight* I will have to give you. It's a pamphlet. Privately printed. We're all born with a fear of falling, understand? But, personally, I feel a fall symbolizes more, a great deal more, than we suspect. I think you'll find it fascinating. Ask the butler for a copy on your way out."

The Underwoods were entranced by the woman. She had an engrossing way with her words and although she was disorganized in her train of thought, she, nonetheless, gave an impression of making sense.

Dolly studied her carefully and she had ample opportunity. For all Gina Langley cared, she and Mrs. Crowley might leave the room whenever they wished. She couldn't have cared less. Gina kept her attention on Charlie for the most part. When she wasn't looking at him directly, she watched the sunning dogs in the garden.

"Actually, what we have at the museum is ordinary."

"I found the work of Mr. Waddington intriguing," chimed Dolly.

"Lars' work is not unknown in this part of the country. That happens to be one of the museum's weaknesses. It has received donations of regional artists. Nothing the scope of, say, *this*." A dramatic gesture took in the room. "But, then, one would never tire of such works. My late husband, Chester, was a superb collector. The Utrillos are the most prized."

"All these paintings are magnificent."

Gina sat up, smiling at young Underwood as she did so.

"You have taste. Where did you learn of art?"

"You mean *about* art?"

"You have a way of suggesting I've said something rude."

"I didn't mean it that way."

Gina laughed gaily and Dolly looked glum.

"Ah," Gina said excitedly, "look at Franco."

She directed their attention to the garden. One of the dogs was carrying on a battle with a pair of dive-bombing mocking birds. "He thinks his garden is Barcelona."

They were strange-looking animals, about four feet in height, gaunt but not thin, with sad piercing eyes and curled tails. All were the color of ash.

Gina caught the Underwoods' curiosity.

"They're Ibizan Hounds. A rare breed."

Charlie looked at them with discernment. "At first I thought they were greyhounds, or, perhaps giant Whippets."

"No, they're Ibizan Hounds. They can outrun a rabbit. I've seen them do it."

"Where was that?"

"In Spain. They're found on the isle of Ibiza. In the Balearic. I've done quite a study on their habits. Originally from Egypt. They're extremely nervous, shy with strangers, but they adore me and I worship them. I think they'll fit in with my Chinese phase. I'm having the entire house redecorated."

"Yes," agreed Charlie, "I imagine they could be considered Asiatic. Asiatic as much as anything else."

"I wanted Chinese Crest dogs," cut in Mrs. Crowley. "Can't have dogs from Spain if everything's coming up Won Ton."

"Chinese Crest dogs," said Gina to no one in particular, "remind me of baby pigs. No matter what phase I choose, baby pigs will not be a part of it."

The atmosphere was uncomfortable. It was the first time that afternoon mother and daughter came close to locking horns.

Dolly asked, "How many dogs do you have?"

"Of this breed?"

"Of the Ibizan Hound, yes."

"Five now. Lorca died a few months ago."

"He wouldn't have died," rasped Mrs. Crowley, "if you hadn't been fooling around with LDS."

This statement made an impact. Gina turned to her mother.

"Get out!"

This was nothing controlled in her order. She meant it and Mrs. Crowley withered.

"Remember what I told you, Mother?"

Mrs. Crowley started to make a protest.

"I've heard enough from you for one day. Now I suggest you leave us alone."

"But—"

"Or shall I call Juan?"

Mrs. Crowley, like some ancient and forgotten matriarch, shuffled from the room, turning once to smirk at her daughter.

"You'll have to forgive Mother. I'm thinking of having her committed. Now, shall we look at the paintings?"

"Mrs. Langley—"

"Gina."

"Gina, we came to ask you about a girl—"

"No need to apologize. I know how much people want to see them. If Michael has sent you then you deserve to view them. Come along. We'll begin with Orozco. My Mexican phase did last too long, but Orozco I kept."

Charlie decided it was not the right time to question the woman regarding Dorothea. He planned to hedge on the subject until Gina might prove more receptive to the topic.

Dolly soon lost interest, but not Charlie. The fact that Charlie's wife wandered about the room by herself didn't disturb Gina; in fact, she preferred it that way, because she didn't much care for females.

On the piano, which was covered with a shawl of Belgian lace, dozens of photos gave testimony to the past, present and future of Gina Langley. (In one she was dressed like an astronaut.) Several were of her early movie days, with the title of the film inked in at the bottom like an artist's signature: *Devil Circus*; *Bed of Silk*; *Are These Our Daughters?* and something called *Honor Has Its Price*. In each photo the charms of Gina were aptly displayed. Whatever she wore, tights, negligee, or peasant costume, she was a lovely woman. Other photos were of her contemporaries: John Gilbert, Mae Murray, Lya de Putti and Erich von Stroheim. The Prussian's photograph displayed just the back of his head with a margin of fat puffing over his stiff collar.

Then there were photographs of Gina with leading artists and writers, and one with Billy Graham. Others were of Gina with men Dolly didn't recognize.

"And now, you have seen my masterpieces," Gina was saying as Dolly returned to them.

"Thank you so much for showing them to us."

"Not at all. When a person, a young man, appreciates what is good in life, he should have every opportunity to express himself."

Now was the moment.

"Interesting sentiment. Mike Jarvits thinks a great deal of you, Mrs. Langley—"

"Gina."

"Gina. And he told me your secretary did, too—before she left. What was her name—Dorothea—Dorothea?"

Gina expressed no surprise or emotion.

"Darnell."

"Yes, Dorothea Darnell."

"This is my favorite Utrillo," Gina said, indicating the painting before them. "A street scene, true. Not my favorite subject, but I think this has something to offer. Howard Stacey informs me you're a private investigator."

Before Charlie could reply, she continued on, "I have always felt that the assumption Utrillo was influenced by Picasso was overdone. I knew him. Maurice."

"Maurice," repeated Dolly.

"Maurice Utrillo."

Dolly felt like a damn fool for the second time that day.

"Yes, Maurice was a devil. An alcoholic by the time he was ten."

"Mrs. Langley—er—Gina—"

"I wonder what that feels like, Charlie, being an alcoholic at ten? The imagery, I suppose, was fantastic, but a condition not likely to be too common. After all, being an alcoholic at ten is indicative of a Latin social malaise. Experience, that's one thing. Did you know that Emperor Nero had his mother and his wife murdered so he could appease the gods and thus find what secrets life and death held?"

She smiled as Charlie's jaw dropped.

"Are you in someone's employ? Is that it?"

Charlie Underwood knew when he had met his match. Gina Langley was a lovely, intelligent woman. The rules of the game would have to be discarded in favor of directness.

"At the moment, no. Miss Lynch suspects someone is threatening Mike. I understand your secretary was referred to as Snow White?"

"I never called her that. Others, I know, did."

"She had a fairy tale quality about her? Hair black as ebony; skin white as snow?"

"I didn't know you had met her."

"Howard Stacey's description."

"Ah, yes, Howard. Bit fanciful for him. I'd say it was more her manner and attitude toward life."

"In what way?"

"Dorothea was a strange girl. She gave everyone sobriquets. How-ard Stacey was Toad of Toad Hall, Carter—that's Carter Aubery—was The Woodcutter. The girl never seemed able to separate life from the book of Grimm's. Why are you interested in *her*?"

"Do you know where she is now living?"

"No, I do not." Gina's tone chilled.

"Have you heard from her?"

"No. Why do you ask?"

"The phone call Mike gets from time to time—"

"Phone call?"

"Yes, someone calls and asks a question—"

Slowly Gina said, "Where is Snow White buried?"

The Underwoods looked at one another.

"Why—why, yes."

Gina paled and sat down beneath an 18th Century miniature by Vestier.

"He's—he's been getting that call?"

"Gina—Gina, have you been getting one?"

She was less herself than at any other time during the past hour.

"One? No, not one. Several"

"A man?"

"Yes, and on my private extension. In my bedroom. Late at night when I'm sleeping. Very few people have that number."

"And what does he say besides asking that damn question?"

"Nothing else at all. I pick up the receiver; the caller asks the ques-tions and then proceeds to cut off."

"And Stacey—has he been getting them?"

"Yes. And Carter Aubery. Lars, too. Lars has had several."

"No idea who the caller might be?"

"None at all." She brightened, rose and started for the double doors.

Charlie asked, "You seem surprised that Mike has had them."

She hadn't regained all her composure, but managed, "I had no idea the list was so lengthy. That's all."

"About your ex-secretary ..."

"I'm afraid I must leave you now, Mr. Underwood. There's a reporter coming to interview me. I head the Phoenix Beautiful Committee, you know. I'll have to change."

Charlie recognized a brush-off when he saw one, but Gina softened it with "I will see you at the funeral?"

"*Funeral?*"

"Actually a memorial service for Henry Ullman. I'm reciting. Please come."

The request sounded like an invitation for cocktails. Charlie felt he should have replied with a "delighted," but "delighted" and a memorial service didn't fit. There were several things he wanted to ask the gracious lady, but they would have to wait.

In the corridor the three were greeted by Mrs. Crowley.

"Leaving so soon, are you? I thought you came for tea!"

She was seated in a simulated balcony a few feet from the floor, looking like a gargoyle of Notre Dame.

"Oh," said Dolly with an embarrassing attempt at a smile. "Howard asked me to give you something for him."

Gina responded, "How nice. What is it?"

"Well—" Dolly fished the stuffed Gila monster from her purse and held it out.

"Ah, yes, the baby Gila monster. Sweet of him."

"You—you want this thing?"

"I'm very interested in desert fauna, Mrs. Underwood. Nothing in creation repulses or disgusts me."

She took the gift.

"Then I will see you two at the service? Four o'clock sharp."

One more try. Charlie said, "You don't know where Snow White—whatever that means exactly—is buried?"

"Remember, four o'clock sharp."

Gina Langley smiled once again, turned and disappeared back into the large gallery room.

They watched Mrs. Crowley hop down from the balcony. She was unique, no doubt about it.

"No tea, huh? Have it your way. Snow White, huh? Don't let Gina kid you. She knows where Snow White is buried, and it ain't in no dwarf's hut."

She grinned, turned and was off on some mysterious errand.

The Underwoods found their own way out after a rather unpleasant scene with the peacock.

Kar—uuu!

Chapter Six

At four the following afternoon, the memorial service for Henry Hector Ullman was ready to commence. All that was needed was the commanding presence of Gina Langley.

The museum had been closed to the public at noon and shortly thereafter florists with their wares began to arrive. Wreaths and bouquets of varied bloom were in profusion, giving off a sickly odor.

Folding chairs had been set out for the mourners, if they could be called that. The physical setting was grimly effective and clinically oppressive.

The Underwoods had taken chairs in the last row. This position gave Charlie an excellent opportunity to see who arrived, and at the same time enabled him to feel inconspicuous. He felt slightly out of place, not having been acquainted with the late lawyer.

The assemblage was a small one: the dearly departed was short on family. Lars Waddington sat toward the front, dressed in a rather flamboyant checked suit and vest, a bright carnation adorning a lapel, his white hair tossed back carelessly from the forehead. He reminded Charlie of photographs he had seen of Max Beerholm, the Greenwich Village poet. Howard Stacey sat next to him, dressed in a drab post-World War II suit of questionable fabric. He appeared fatigued. Mike and Lisa arrived late, waved to the Underwoods guiltily and quickly took chairs.

Charlie and Dolly were both cognizant of a long, thin man with a fleshless face and pronounced Adam's apple.

Carter Aubery.

The jetting from his throat bounced spasmodically, and they found it rather difficult not to watch the jumping action.

That he was possessed was quite evident. His eyes were deep set and haunted, like something from one of Waddington's works. He fancied the anachronism of a walking stick. He sat alone, in a section of chairs off to one side, as if he were the sole member of the surviving family.

There were a few others; people who worked at the museum, and also the detective from Police Headquarters, Tod Van Spanckeren. His presence struck Charlie as peculiar.

Organ music was piped in from somewhere. Brahms. They were seated in a section of the first floor. A permanent partition separated the memorial area from the scene of Ullman's misfortune, splitting the large room in two, although it didn't go from floor to ceiling and had openings, here and there, for the placement of *objets d'art*.

The lighting dimmed and a baby spot picked out a table hosting a vase containing a single red rose.

A stirring went through the gathering. Gina Langley was descending a staircase. She wore white, gossamer and eye-catching, and the garment clung to her body sensuously. She took a step at a time, catlike and poised. Her auburn hair was done in such a manner that from a distance she looked no more than sixteen. Several steps behind, making the descent in a most inelegant fashion, stumbled along Mrs. Crowley. Dolly was relieved that the mourners were spared the Chinese phase, at least for the duration of the service.

Mrs. Crowley had chosen to go traditional: black veil, black dress and shoes. The works. The poor woman had trouble making her way in the dimness and she was further burdened by the large, cumbersome urn she carried.

The remains of the late Hank Ullman.

Gina reached the table and paused by the rose, which she plucked from the vase, lifted to her nostrils and inhaled. A smile, vague but contented, crept across her lips. Mrs. Crowley missed a step and grumbled something in bad taste.

Everyone pretended they hadn't heard.

"Here," said Gina, aloof and distant, "place Henry here. On the table. By me."

Mrs. Crowley hurried to the table, and with a sigh of relief banged the urn to the table, rolled the veil, which had been tucked over the hat's brim, down over her wrinkled face, and sat with an audible *plump* in the first row.

A white-gloved hand was raised and the Brahms faded delicately to silence.

Gina put the rose down, shut her eyes for a moment, and then began:

"Life is a fragment, a brief eternity between eternities. A moment. This rose petal to a larger rose; death a petal to a larger life. Men are matter and matter does not die. Never . . ."

She droned on in this manner for about ten minutes. Neither Charlie nor Dolly could make heads or tails of what she was saying. Charlie remembered that he'd forgotten to ask the butler for a copy of *Flight*. A credit to Gina's ability as an actress, no one moved noticeably while she spoke. She looked elegant, soulful. The rose played its role dramatically, too. Occasionally Gina referred to it, stressing some obscure point.

The room was becoming uncomfortably warm. A guard was quietly opening air-conditioning vents and Charlie suddenly became excited. He watched the man with interest. Gina passed temporarily from his thoughts.

The vents were located in several spots along the walls; some were quite high, out of reach for arm's length. The guard carried a short pole with a brass hook at the end. This enabled him to hoist the hook to the vent and either close or open it. He was able to avoid leaving the memorial section of the room merely by jetting the pole through an opening in the wall and making contact on the opposite side.

Charlie was once again conscious of Gina Langley's voice. She was bringing the rose to her bosom, her words softening, her eyes closing. Tighter and tighter her hands swallowed the flower, until she had crushed it utterly and the petals fell like pinkish snow to the table top.

Dolly could contain herself no longer. "She's—she's magnificent." She turned to Charlie. He was pale.

"Charlie?" She nudged him. "Charlie, Gina is a great actress."

"I've discovered something, too," he answered, in a tone close to a whisper.

"What's that, dear?"

"How Henry Ullman was murdered."

Dolly wasn't convinced she had heard correctly; then she was positive she had.

"Charlie?"

He studied the radiant Gina with more than routine interest.

"Not now. Later."

"But, Charlie—"

"Later."

The lighting rose to fullness and people began to cough and murmur.

"Not bad!" bellowed Mrs. Crowley. "Now what are you going to do with Hanky boy?"

It was as if no one had heard. Gina waved toward the guard. He placed the pole against the partition wall and walked to the table. Gina indicated the urn.

"To the Shelly Room."

He nodded, picked up the silver container and climbed the stairs.

"Didn't expect you here."

Charlie turned and found himself staring into the face of Tod Van Spanckeren, a countenance that appeared shaven to the bone of its leanness.

"That might go for you, too. You were a friend of Henry Ullman?"

"In a way."

He was smiling at Dolly.

"This is Inspector Van Spanckeren, Dolly. Tod—my wife."

Dolly smiled brightly and the policeman passed a few pleasantries regarding the Arizona climate. He excused himself and went to speak with Carter Aubery.

"Charlie, what is this about discovering how Ullman was murdered. Why didn't you tell Tod?"

"All in good time."

"But, Charlie—"

A weary look from her husband silenced her protests. She had seen that expression many times before. Once, in a desolate mountain resort in Liechtenstein, it foreshadowed the unraveling of some fairly enigmatic events.

Lisa came walking over toward her old friend. She didn't look at all well, rather drawn and exhausted.

"I–I didn't know you were planning to come. We could have ridden together. The four of us."

Dolly said, "I don't think Mike would go for that."

"He–he told me he came out to see you. He wants to apologize. I know he does, but he's embarrassed."

"Did you tell him you had asked me to do a bit of investigating?"

She shook her head, "No, of course not. I think it was Howard. He's something of an old woman when it comes to keeping his mouth shut."

Charlie said, "I must be slipping. I wasn't aware I had told Howard I was investigating anything."

"Doesn't matter with him," replied Lisa, "he's one of those people who adore keeping the phone buzzing."

Charlie and Dolly caught the significance.

"Oh," Lisa hastened, "I don't mean that weird phone business, only that he's something of a gossip. Wants so bad to fit in with this group and feels he's on the outside. That's why he told Mike, I imagine."

Dolly asked "How are the wedding plans progressing?"

"I guess they're progressing. Mike, he hasn't—"

Her words were cut off by the arrival of Carter Aubery. On close inspection he looked even more haggard than when the Underwoods first took note of him. Like a well-groomed corpse. The Adam's apple bounced and then he said to Lisa, "These are your friends from New England?"

"Yes, Carter. You didn't meet them at the opening?"

"If I had met them at the opening, I'd hardly ask my question."

If Lisa was offended by Aubery's rudeness, she concealed her attitude. Dolly figured her friend had worked out her relationship with the "in" group and hence knew precisely where she stood.

"You'll forgive me, Carter. I thought you had met. May I present my old friend, Dolly Underwood and her husband, Charlie."

Aubery extended his hand in greeting.

"Mr. Underwood," he said stiffly, then nodded with a curt bow of the head to Dolly, and the Adam's apple did an up and down.

"I wonder," said Aubery to Charlie, "if I might have a word with you?"

"Why, yes, of course."

Carter Aubery walked ahead toward a small room not far from the reception desk. The two men entered and Aubery offered Charlie a chair, then closed the door.

The "mourners" showed no sign of leaving the museum.

Standing, Aubery said directly, "You're a private detective?"

Charlie laughed, not unkindly. "No secret if that is what you are implying."

"I never imply."

"What you mean, Carter—"

"Mr. Aubery."

"Fine by me. What you mean, Mr. Aubery, is—am I employed by someone at the moment? Someone connected with the museum?"

"Exactly."

"No, I am not."

"Gina, dear Gina," he said with a tinge of sarcasm, "informs me that you know of the phone calls. Those awful annoying rings."

"I do."

"Have you found out anything about them?"

"Nothing, except many people are receiving them."

"I can recite the list. What interests me is the theory that one Michael Jarvits is receiving them, as well."

"A theory?"

Carter Aubery walked toward the far end of the room, turned, and with his hands folded behind his back, began to retrace his steps.

"You are not employed?" He seemed defiant and a little scared.

"At the moment. Correct."

"You are here in the Valley of the Sun on a holiday? You were not sent for?"

"Also correct. On both points. My wife and Miss Lynch are old friends."

"I see. How much longer do you intend to remain?"

Charlie had had enough.

"I intend to remain as long as I choose. Be it one day or one month more," he answered rather angrily.

"Would you take on an assignment if one were offered?"

"That would depend on a number of factors."

"Explain yourself."

"What the assignment happened to be. My disposition. Finances."

"Ah, yes, always finances."

Carter Aubery stated a figure.

"I will want to see you this evening, Mr. Underwood. At my apartment. Camelback Towers. Some time between eleven and twelve. I work there until that hour. After that I drink and attempt to relax. Come then. Alone."

"Without my wife, you mean."

"I mean precisely what I said. *Alone*."

"Very well," announced Charlie, rising from his chair. "At your apartment. Tonight. Camelback Towers."

He opened the door to discover Tod Van Spanckeren leaning against the wall.

"You know," said Charlie with a phony drawl, "if I didn't know better, I'd suspect you was trailin' me, pardner."

"It may look that way."

Museum attendants had carried a table into the lobby, with flowers, plates of cookies and several bottles of wines.

The two detectives walked in this direction as they spoke.

"Remember," said Tod, "you weren't going to step on any toes."

"I'm not likely to forget. Has someone been screaming 'ouch'?"

"Not yet. You were going to let me know if you stumbled on anything of interest."

"I'm beginning to think this is one hell of a vacation."

"If you do hit something, remember I'm on your side."

"What is that supposed to mean? And what, exactly, are you doing here?"

"Keeping an eye on things. Nothing more."

Gina was pouring wine for the mourners and Charlie stepped to the table.

"Ah, it's Charlie. That light brown suit becomes you. But there's too much red in your tie. With that suit might I suggest a touch of yellow? Men, after all, were meant to have gay plumage."

She smiled graciously and handed him a glass of sherry. He looked at the table with something of a questioning glance.

"You have the look of a censor, Charles."

"Not really."

"The funeral feast; the wedding banquet."

She looked in the direction of Mike and Lisa.

"We take death far too seriously. Life is the thing to be concerned with, not death. The living, not the dead. That's why I wear white today. In some countries white symbolizes mourning, but that's not why I put on this frock. When I awoke this morning I felt pure, symbolically virginal, consequently I dress to fit my—"

"Phase?"

"*Mood*. One can have a mood within a phase, but never the other way around. Imbalance like immoderation is unaesthetic. You have met Mr. Jenckes?"

She indicated the man standing beside her.

"No, I haven't had the pleasure."

The two men shook hands.

"Mr. Jenckes was Henry Ullman's law partner. The museum is now his responsibility."

"Quite a responsibility, too," the lawyer said.

"I'm sure you can handle it in Aces, Mr. Jenckes," Charlie said in way of conversation.

Mr. Jenckes replied, "I won't be sitting under any statues, I can tell you that." This was said without malice, almost kindly.

Mr. Jenckes shrugged his shoulders with a sly, knowing look.

He was a pleasant-looking chap and Charlie wondered how he had gotten along with his late law partner.

Dolly joined him.

"Gina, I thought your eulogy was moving."

"So did I, Mrs. Underwood."

She handed Dolly a glass of wine and moved toward Lars Waddington, who, along with Howard Stacey, was polishing off a plate of almond cookies.

With a pastry in one hand and a glass of wine in the other, it was difficult for Dolly to realize the purpose of the gathering.

"I'm surprised," she said to Charlie in a low voice, "that they removed the urn. Considering everything, I'd have thought he'd have made for a good centerpiece."

"Maybe they'll bring him back."

The pastry in Dolly's mouth suddenly tasted dry and bitter.

Mike Jarvits was walking toward them, an expression of guilt on his youthful face. When he was directly in front of the Underwoods, he held out his hand in apology, like an unruly school boy brought to heel.

"Sorry about the other evening, Charlie. I guess my emotion got the best of me. Now, I understand, you know we've all been getting the messages."

"I don't know about all. Who *all* might be. But I know several of the people connected with the museum have."

"My behavior was boorish. I hope you'll accept my apology."

The change in temperament was more than marked, as if Mike were boldly attempting to get on the good side of Charlie.

Half an hour later the museum was opened to the public. The table was cleared and the mourners began to leave.

"Charlie, if you don't tell me what you've discovered, I'll burst with curiosity."

Charlie took his wife by the arm and pulled her along the side of the partition wall.

He spoke softly, not wishing anyone to overhear; someone who might come in their direction.

"Remember, Dolly, the weight of the bronze made it difficult to move."

"Naturally."

"The murderer—"

"The murderer?" She said this in a rush of breath.

"Be quiet, baby. The murderer wasn't standing anywhere near the statue." He picked up the pole that the guard, earlier that afternoon, had used to unhook the vents, and angled it through the statuary niche in the wall."

Neatly, perfectly, the hook of the pole touched a bronze casting on the opposite side. Dolly understood the maneuver.

"All the murderer had to do," she whispered, "was unhook the steel bar at one time or other and wait for his chance."

"Correct. The museum's opening was so mobbed that no one could tell who was standing on the opposite side of the wall. Everyone thought that the pushing came from the Ullman side."

Tod Van Spanckeren approached. Charlie stood the pole against the wall.

"I'm leaving," the police inspector said politely. "A pleasure to meet you, Mrs. Underwood."

Dolly smiled.

"I'll be in touch, Charlie."

Van Spanckeren turned, caught sight of the pole and paused. The Underwoods held their breath as he took hold of the thing.

"Something like a javelin. I used to be a fine javelin thrower."

He handled the hooked pole like an athlete.

"'Course I couldn't hit a mark with something like this. Nothing worth hitting, that is. Poor balance."

Chapter Seven

Dolly was restless.

She had watched television disinterestedly for some forty-five minutes, ever since Charlie left on his rendezvous with Carter Aubery. To relieve her boredom, she had put on a delicious nightgown of pink fluff that came only to about twelve inches above her attractive knees. Her small feet were warmed by bunny slippers. Silly-looking things, a weakness of hers. She rarely wore them when Charlie was around, for he kidded her about them.

She had wanted to go with him, promising she'd wait faithfully in the car, but Charlie had nixed this idea. Carter Aubery was insistent that Charlie come solo and the detective was determined to honor this request. Still, Dolly never relished being alone. She liked people and most people returned the compliment. Even Gina, who didn't like women at all, was civil.

What prompted the sexy nightgown and babyish booties were the antics of the Leopard Woman. She was on the terrace having late cocktails with a short, dumpy gentleman who puffed a long black cigar. Dolly wanted to think the worst, so she did.

Once in the nightie, Dolly studied her shape in the mirror, deciding that the Leopard Woman had nothing, but *nothing*, that she herself didn't possess. The lady on the terrace was freer with it—that was all.

Television had been a bore. One channel presented the antics of two sarcastic crows with Cockney accents, another (the educational channel) a lecture on paper flowers; a western and a panel show rounded out the dreary entertainment.

The phone rang. Dolly was delighted.

"Hello," she said eagerly, hoping Charlie was telling her to get a cab and come zooming into town.

It was just the room clerk.

"Mrs. Underwood," came his voice, vacant and professional.

"Yes."

"A Mrs. Crowley to see you."

"Who?"

"Crowley, a Mrs. Crowley."

"Ask her to come down."

"Yes, Mrs. Underwood."

Dolly took a robe from the closet and put it on. She lit a cigarette and opened the cabana's door, so the old woman would be able to find the room.

In a minute or so, on the terrace, appeared Mrs. Crowley, a sort of latter-day Miss Haversham, demented, but arresting. In her arms she was carrying a freakish dog of some kind.

"Here, Mrs. Crowley," Dolly shouted as the woman started to make a wrong turn.

"Howdy-doo, howdy-doo."

"Howdy—I mean, how are you?"

"I've been better. I brought along Fu Manchu."

"Your little dog?"

"Ain't a make of egg roll."

She was in the room. "Where's your husband? I have to speak with him."

Dolly left the door ajar. "You missed him. He had to go into town. Business."

"Monkey or legit?"

Mrs. Crowley sat down, taking in the room as she did.

"Legit—I mean, it was a business appointment. Is this one of those Ibizan dogs?"

"Fu man? No this is a Chinese Crest. Went out and bought him today. One hundred and fifty-two bucks. Two bucks for the license or something. Understand?"

"Why—I think I do."

"How come you're dressed in that robe?"

"It's very late. I thought I'd be going to bed shortly."

"Can't have a drink with you in that. Won't let us in the bar. I know these resort hangouts. Narrow-minded."

"Charlie keeps a bottle if you care for something. Whiskey."

"So I drink whiskey. Little water to wash it down."

Dolly poured a pony of whiskey and handed the shot glass to the woman. She downed the liquor quickly and accepted the glass of water Dolly offered with a muffled, "Thanks."

"Your husband found out about Snow White yet?"

"Not that I know of."

"Let me tell you something. I know that museum bunch. Understand? Nutty as I am, I'm plain everyday cuckoo. Garden variety. Gina's the real stuff. Don't find them like her too often."

"We were talking about Snow White—"

"No, we weren't. I was telling you about her."

"Yes, that right—"

"She was a kook, too. Minute I laid eyes on her I figured she was straight from the happy farm. My Gina can pick 'em. Anyway, she wandered around the house like she was a sleepwalker, but I knew her. Made a pass for every man that came into the place. Always wore funny clothes. Ever met a woman like that?"

"I – I—"

It was an uncomfortable predicament. The Chinese phase had

obviously been reinstated: Mrs. Crowley was attired in a billowy coat of exquisite design. The coat did a lot for her; she did nothing for it and she did look "funny."

"Simple black dress. White dickie collar. That jazz. Thought she was June Allyson."

"She had many boyfriends?"

"Boyfriends? Don't know nothing about boyfriends. She knew plenty of elder gents, sad-faced johns who should have known better. That's why I'm here. I think someone bumped her off."

"Bumped her-off—?"

"Did her in. That day—the day she didn't show—everyone was acting mighty cute. Even Gina. And she don't have to *act* cute. That girl was shaken. Said it was because Lorca died. Got hit by Dorothea's car. Gina said that's why she blew; Dorothea didn't want to face her. Gina was nuts over that dog."

"You – you don't believe that?"

"Sweetie, I'm not much of a fool. I've got a good life. Gina and me. Now, I'll tell you what I think. Someone's blackmailing my baby. That's what I think. I think Snow White has found a home in a glass casket. I don't know how she got her chips, but I think someone's finished her off. Somehow Gina's mixed up in it, but I don't know how."

She put the hairless dog down on the floor.

"He wouldn't piddle."

Mrs. Crowley opened her bag, a large one covered with a design of strung seashells.

"What a beautiful handbag."

"Yeah, from Shanghai or Shangri-la—some far-out place like that." She took out a checkbook.

"I'll make out a check for five hundred. Five hundred more when Charlie finds out who's bothering my little girl."

"Who do you think would have killed her?"

"What do you think I'm employing your man for?"

"But you have no real proof or anything."

"Listen, Bright Eyes, I've been hugging close to this terrain for more years than I care to remember. When I smell a rat, I smell a rat. Don't let Gina's sweet pussycat smile and fancy lip turn you off. She's plenty scared. I don't like that. Haven't seen that old broad cry for the last twenty years. She was crying last night. Another one of those phone calls."

"I see. Shall I have Charlie call you when he comes in?"

"Not unless he's got something to report."

"I'll tell him everything you've said."

"I hope so," the old woman said, perturbed, "I haven't been beating the breeze for nothing. Tell him to call in a day or so in any case. There may be another one of those phone calls."

"Yes, yes, I'll do that."

Fu Manchu ran under the bed. Mrs. Crowley attempted to coax him out, with no success. Dolly captured him and handed him to his new mistress. She thought him an incredibly ugly puppy, agreeing with Gina's description of "little pig."

"Remember," admonished Mrs. Crowley leaving the cabana, "Mum's the word."

This struck her as amusing and she repeated it. "Mum's the word. Not bad for a song title. I used to write the things you know."

She waved a gloved hand in goodbye, and headed for the terrace steps, the Chinese Crest yelping indignantly. Dolly closed the door and looked at the check. She gave a forlorn sigh.

Mrs. Crowley had forgotten to sign the retainer.

Camelback Towers was a high-rise building on Phoenix's main artery, North Central Avenue. When first built it was considered ultra-fashionable, a situation due to its status as the sole multi-storied building on the stretch.

It was eleven o'clock to the stroke when Charlie Underwood began his ascent. Aubery's apartment was the entire top floor. There was a balcony that stretched in front of the elevator, and it gave Charlie an opportunity to view the surrounding city from his eerie perch.

In all directions flickering lights darted to and fro, like bits on a strand of electric pearls. Dark mountain shapes edged toward the star-dotted heavens and the atmosphere was calm and peaceful. He wasn't cognizant of the music that drifted from Aubery's apartment until it hit a crescendo. He walked to the apartment door and rang.

He had to push on the buzzer several times, because the music was being played at a high volume. At last, the door finally opened.

Carter Aubery, eyes haunted, drink in hand, looked genuinely pleased to see the detective.

"Eleven I take it," he said in greeting.

"After."

"Come in, Mr. Underwood, won't you?"

Entering was like walking into Gina's museum room all over again. Carter Aubery's collection wasn't as catholic as Gina's but it, too, was breathtaking, and the apartment's occupant seemed delighted with Charlie's silent admiration.

"I've been told you know something about paintings."

"Some, but I'm beginning to think this city has the corner on masterpieces. I've seen what Gina has."

"Many of mine are equally as good. On occasion, we trade."

"*Trade?*"

"If I have something she wants badly, then I usually find something at her place that takes my fancy and—"

"You—er—trade."

Carter Aubery made an attempt at smiling. He failed.

"You find that unusual?"

"I guess," said Charlie with a perspective gleam in his eye, "it depends on the circles you travel in. When I was a kid we used to trade comics. A *Superman* for a *Wonder Woman*, things like that."

Carter tried to laugh, "Oh, yes, I see. Droll. Very droll, indeed. You mean there's a correlation between that and swapping a Gauguin for a

Chagall? Interesting. Extremely. I imagine Freud would support your theory. We're all children at heart. All children. Sounds biblical, doesn't it?"

Charlie thought: People connected with the Memorial Museum would have done well at the Mad Hatter's Tea Party. He felt a cold chill run up and down his spine as he realized he was thinking in the vein of a Dorothea Darnell.

Carter said pleasantly, "You will have a drink? Private detectives do drink. On duty?"

"And off."

"Splendid. I'm highly suspicious of people who never take a drink. Usually covering up for one guilt or another. Appearing holier than thou—understand?"

"Yes, I do."

Charlie didn't. Not all the way. But he let it pass.

Carter Aubery had led the way from the foyer to the living room, a thick-carpeted, sunken affair, encased on three sides by floor-to-ceiling windows. Additional paintings completely covered the one non-glass wall.

The bar was a lengthy cabinet of teak.

Carter appeared relaxed and this pleased Charlie, for he had the idea Carter would turn out to be an intense neurotic, difficult to talk with, impossible to predict his actions.

"What will it be?"

"Scotch."

"Excellent. I'm drinking the same. We share similar tastes. In liquor. That's a start, that's a start."

Charlie took a few steps back from the living room, close to the foyer and began to investigate the paintings. Most were by artists he knew nothing of, but he spotted two Waddingtons and a Cezanne. He was captured by the technique and subject matter exhibited by three of the paintings.

Carter brought Charlie his drink.

"On the rocks, right?"

"Yes," Charlie lied. (He liked water as a mix—not too much, but enough to color the flavor.)

"You're looking at Beckmann. Do you like his work?"

"I'm afraid I don't know of him," Charlie said, sipping his Scotch.

"I'm disappointed." He seemed sincere. "Beckmann, Max Beckmann was a genius. Not for everyone's taste. Something like Waddington. Lars' works terrify most people. He paints their secrets. People don't appreciate that. Personally, I believe we should be able to face anything."

There was more meaning in Aubery's last statement than he intended. Charlie caught the slip. Aubery continued on, "Max died shortly after the war. I knew him."

"Did you? Gina tells me she knew Utrillo."

"Gina has known everyone."

"Max was terribly bitter about the Third Reich. Works in symbols."

Carter looked at Charlie slyly and moved a few steps along the wall, passing as he did so, a Picasso, a Gauguin, a Renoir, another Waddington. He stopped before another Beckman.

This one was executed in washes of brown, the figures isolated. The pivotal figure was a young woman, tall in proportion to the work's dimension. The background was taken by stunted creatures compressed in space so their features were cruelly distorted. There was more to this painting than the direct expression of its creator. There was no mistaking the subject matter: Snow White and the Seven Dwarfs.

"What do you think?"

"I think Herr Beckmann a striking craftsman."

"You appreciate this one, then?"

"Like Waddington's work, I'd say it depends entirely on personal reaction. The subject matter. Technically, there's no denying the man has talent."

Aubery gave an outburst of loud, piercing laughter.

"Look at the name! Look at the name!"

Charlie didn't understand.

"The name! The name! The signature on the painting."

Charlie looked closely, reading: Carter Aubery.

"I'm confused. You—you're Max Beckmann?"

"No, not me. I've copied his style. Beckmann's."

"You've done a masterful job."

"Thank you. To be truthful, I didn't believe Gina when she said the drug would free my inner-creativity. Works only with people who are basically creative, you understand. And if I hadn't had sufficient knowledge of this particular artist and his approach to painting, I wouldn't have been able to do it. No, not at all."

"What drug?"

"I beg your pardon?"

"Drug. You mentioned a drug."

An expression of uneasiness came over Carter's face.

"Not important. Shall we discuss business?"

They returned to the living room and took seats. One section of the room was occupied by a large desk. Here magazines, newspapers, clippings and photographs were neatly stacked.

"You work at home?" queried Charles.

"Most of the time. I dislike office routine. Most of my work I do on the telephone."

Carter began to explain the workings of his magazine, a publication devoted to expounding the joys of desert living.

"Never made any money. I have to subsidize the thing."

Charlie looked at several issues spread out on a coffee table by his chair. *Arrowheads* was a stunning publication, glossy and well illustrated.

Carter was dressed in a handsome Indian shirt. His trousers were linen, but he wore no shoes or socks.

"I have reason to suspect that Mike Jarvits is at the bottom of these vicious calls."

Charlie was aghast.

"I thought," said Carter coolly, "private detectives—"

"Investigator—"

"Private investigators showed no emotion."

"We have emotion, Mr. Aubery. You threw me for a moment, however. I won't deny that. And why, do you think, Jarvits is the culprit?"

Blandly he replied, "He and Dorothea were lovers."

"You have proof?"

"I've been reliably informed."

"By whom?"

"I'd rather not divulge my source of information. At this time, anyway."

"But you do believe your informant?"

"Implicitly."

"All right," said Charlie draining his glass. "Suppose this is true— assumption. Why would he plague you with such a cruel hoax?"

"Dorothea is gone. I knew her. Yes—" His tone got softer. "I knew her, too. The point is, I believe, Mr. Jarvits suspects I've murdered the girl."

This time Charlie was prepared for the revelation. "I see. Why?"

"Before Mr. Jarvits, Dorothea and I—the flesh is a poor judge of character. Broken off months ago. One day Dorothea disappears. She was making things uncomfortable for me, I won't deny that. I had reason to want her out of the way. Jarvits suspects I've killed her."

"You're not alone in getting the calls."

"I think that's camouflage. I'm the one he's after."

"Your informant again?"

"Yes."

"Then you think Jarvits was in love with her—enough for revenge?"

"What is 'in love with her—enough'? You see, I never wanted the man in the museum. Took a distinct dislike to him. The museum was to be ours. I mean Gina's, mine, Henry's—and this Jarvits has plans for it. Turning it into a civic enterprise. I believe Gina was developing a fondness for this idea. If Gina turned it over to the city he'd be in a fine position to head it as curator-director. I'm safe in assuming he's working on Gina with the absurdity."

"What about Howard Stacey?"

"Kicked upstairs so we could get the city's support—no taxes—that sort of arrangement. I told Gina I wasn't going to donate any of my works if the museum was going to be handed over to the municipal authorities. I also told her I'd change the clause in my will--"

"Clause?"

"Should I die, all my paintings go to Gina. Should *she* die, I receive all of hers."

"I see."

"Can you be of help?"

"You want me to investigate Jarvits? Determine if *he* is the caller?"

"Precisely. Also I want you to see that he doesn't attempt to blackmail me about my relationship with Dorothea. Above all, that he makes no attempt to kill me."

Charlie stood.

"You're presenting me with two men, you realize that?"

"No."

"On one hand you're intimating that Mike Jarvits is some kind of blackmailer, soon to show his hand."

"Yes."

"On the other hand you're presenting him as some kind of love-crazed lunatic, bent on terrorizing you for doing away with his sweetheart."

Carter Aubery sighed deeply and turned his eyes from Charlie. "I see no inconsistency. Either way I am a victim, am I not?"

"Carter—"

"Mr. Aubery. I dislike familiarity."

"*Carter*," repeated Charlie and Aubery said nothing, "I would like the name of your informant."

"I cannot give you that information. That's a condition should you decide to take this case. You will take it, won't you? I need your assistance."

"Why not the police?"

"Be sensible. I don't want any notoriety."

"I shall have to think about it, Carter."

"If you prove it's Mr. Jarvits, there'll be a bonus for you."

Charlie nodded goodnight and started out.

"Allow me to show you out."

"Not necessary," said Charlie as he passed the paintings, recalling their earlier conversation about comic books. "I'm a big boy now."

Chapter Eight

It was the hour after dawn, when the stillness of early morning is unearthly.

Charlie was awake. For rest, it had been a bad night. Dolly was asleep when he had returned. He had wanted to wake her, but thought better of it. Instead, he smoked several cigarettes sitting by the pool's edge. Some things were beginning to focus, but the whole affair remained, basically, an enigma.

About 3 a.m. he had crawled beneath the sheets and kissed his young wife on the nape of her lovely neck. She moved in her sleep, one arm along the pillows, but she didn't waken.

Charlie had closed his eyes. Nothing happened. He tossed and turned. Finally, he left his bed, dressed and returned to the pool's edge.

The surface of the water was calm, mysteriously placid, not a ripple. It would be hours before the attendants, armed with long brushes, would begin their chores around the pool, stretching out the brushes to skim any impurities from the mirror-like stillness.

What troubled Charlie weren't the things people said, rather their omissions. Who, for example, was the person who told Carter that Dorothea and Mike were lovers? And what reason would Carter have for not revealing the name, unless there was no informant? Had Aubery deliberately lied so Charlie would not suspect he was working solely on personal belief?

He hammered at this theory, an hour later, when Dolly was up and showering.

"Then you think Carter Aubery suspects Mike on his own? The informer is a sham?"

The rush of water made her speak in a shout.

"Could be," replied Charlie.

"You're not sure?"

"Baby, I'm not sure of *nothing.*"

"Brace yourself," came the voice from the stall.

"Huh?"

"I've some news."

Charlie stepped to the shower stall and caught a fetching glimpse of his wife, silhouetted in a steamy fashion behind the transparent door.

"I've got a terrific idea," he said.

"What?"

She turned off the water and sheepishly opened the door.

"Sorry, sweetheart," she said with a wry grin, "didn't hear what you said."

"I said," he repeated, taking a large fluffy towel from a holder, "that I've got a terrific idea. I'm going to buy that door and sell it to disappointed husbands."

She looked puzzled.

"See, baby, it'll be your figure the gentlemen will see when their wives are showering. They can dream."

Dolly laughed. She liked the idea.

Charlie laughed, too. Dolly told him about Mrs. Crowley's visit. He stopped laughing.

"First time," he said with seriousness, "I've ever been engaged by three people, for basically the same reason, at the same time."

Dolly slipped on a terrycloth robe. Actually it was Charlie's, but she fancied the wrapper's bulkiness after a shower.

"That would be Lisa, Mrs. Crowley and Aubery?"

"Correct," he said, sitting down.

Dolly sat on the edge of the bed.

"But," she interjected, "you can't really count Lisa, can you? I mean—"

"She's not paying me, if that's what you mean."

"Neither is Miss Chinatown 1901. She forgot to sign the check. Darling, shouldn't you try to sleep?"

"I wish I could but I can't. I'm holding up nicely."

"Let me call room service and we can have breakfast here in the cabana."

"No objection."

She called and gave the order.

"One thing is decided. I can't keep it secret much longer. From the police."

"How Ullman was killed?"

"Yes. I'll have to call Van Spanckeren today."

"With *his* eyes he could be dangerous."

"He seemed to like you?"

"Perhaps I ought to send you whenever I have anything to discuss with him."

She stuck her tongue out at him.

"Okay," Charlie said without taking notice. "Ullman was murdered. Check point one. That much we know. We also know that several people are receiving mysterious phone calls asking the question, 'Where is Snow White buried?' Do you know who these people are, Dolly? What they share in common?"

She was running a comb through her hair.

"That's easy; they're all connected with the museum."

"True, but there's a closer tie than that. After all, many, many people are connected with the museum in one way or another."

She paused in her combing. "Let me think a minute. Mike's been getting them. We have Lisa's word on that."

Dolly saw the analytical gleam in her husband's eye.

"Oh, Charlie, you don't think Lisa's lying—why should she?"

"Go on, baby. Mike's been getting them. Who else?"

"Gina."

"Correct."

"Ah—let me think … Ah—*Carter*! Carter Aubery."

"Brilliant. Now, what committee do they all, save Mike, serve on? At the museum?"

Dolly toyed with the comb distractedly. Her eyes brightened.

"Why, each serves on the board of directors."

"Bingo!"

She wore a broad smile that gradually faded as she thought over her conclusion.

"But there are other people on that board. What about—Howard Stacey?"

"When we saw him at his studio and mentioned 'Snow White' he said nothing about any calls. This could mean one of two things. He preferred not to let on he was getting them or else—simply—he wasn't."

Dolly said: "No one else was hesitant about admitting them. Everyone on the board has been getting them, you think?"

"I think they've either been getting them or they've been gotten out of the way."

Dolly pressed her lips in concentration.

"Ullman was a board member. He was murdered. Dorothea was a board member and she's dropped from sight, but not from mind. Howard is the only person who has not admitted receiving them."

"Are you thinking that Howard might have murdered Ullman?"

"I'm not thinking anything. I'm trying to, though."

"I'm glad of that," beamed Dolly a shade smugly, "because you've left out someone."

Charlie consulted his notebook.

"What about my visitor last evening? Wasn't she a board member?"

Charlie sighed. "Right you are. She's on the board. Okay—Howard and Mrs. Crowley unaccounted for."

"Are you going to tell Tod?"

"For the time being, just about Ullman. You know, Gina was surprised Mike was getting the calls. As if she felt along the lines of Carter—that Mike was responsible for them."

"I wonder if Lisa knows about Dorothea and Mike. That might have been the reason she blew up the time I mentioned the Darnell name."

"A possibility. 'Course Jarvits did a fast turnabout at the memorial service yesterday. He may be telling the truth when he said he didn't know anyone else was getting the anonymous calls. Still, he was so adamant earlier—"

"That *was* strange—that switch in temperament."

Charlie was doodling, a habit he had when deducing.

"That question about 'Snow White' is more than interesting. The implication is that Dorothea is dead and secretly buried. Aubery said Dorothea knew a great deal about his private life."

Dolly added, "So did Mrs. Crowley—Dorothea knows so much about Gina, I mean. Whatever there was to *know*. Dorothea, according to that old dame, was a potential blackmailer among other things."

Charlie doodled a caricature of Mrs. Crowley.

"Do you recall what Mrs. Crowley said to Gina about Lorca?"

"*Lorca?*"

"One of those hounds."

"That's right. His name came up in the conversation last night. No, I don't remember exactly, although I recall it started some unpleasant exchange."

"She said Lorca never would have died if Gina hadn't been fooling around with LDS. What do those letters mean to you?"

Dolly repeated the letters, "L-D-S, L-D-S – I know--!" Her jubilant expression melted. "That doesn't make sense. LDS stands for Latter Day Saints, doesn't it?"

Charlie nodded assent: "Yes—Mormons."

Dolly rose and went to the closet to select a morning dress. "That's a good one. A dog wouldn't have died if Gina hadn't been involved with the Mormon Church."

"A stickler, okay."

"Yet, you can't pay much attention to her, dear. She's close to eighty if she's not there already. Remarkably spry. I think she's a wonder, but she is confused. Like not signing the check. Or maybe that's plain cleverness."

"I think," Charlie said, "you might visit with your old friend again. Lisa. Be smooth. See if you can get anything out of her about Mike and Dorothea. You might catch something that's slipped by me."

"Aye, aye, captain." She saluted.

"That Aubery. What paintings! Gina and Carter combined could corner the art market. He's not bad himself. He's done a painting in the style of a German artist, Max Beckmann—ever hear of him?"

"Can't say that I have."

"The reproduction of style and technique is masterly. Said he owed it to Gina. She had told him about some drug that—oh—how did he put it?—*Frees inner creativity*—something like that. Didn't want to talk about it. Strange man."

"So far you haven't discovered much except how Ullman was murdered."

"More than that. We know who 'Snow White' is or was, and we know people thought she was not above blackmail. Some people, Mr. Carter and Mrs. Crowley. Another odd thing—about those two—they swap masterpieces like ice cream cones."

A knock.

Charlie opened the door to the steward, thanked and tipped him.

They sat at the table.

Picking up on their conversation, Dolly said, "When's the last time you swapped an ice cream cone?"

She leaned toward him and kissed his cheek. They turned their attention to breakfast.

The phone rang shortly after eleven. Dolly had decided on a dip and was gaily playing the role of porpoise in a pool when its insistent *r–r–ring* woke Charlie from a deep, exhausted sleep.

"Underwood?" came the voice at the other end.

Since he was not fully awake, he had difficulty understanding what was being said. He managed, "Underwood—yeah, yeah, Charlie Underwood."

The voice again, "What? Anything the matter?"

"Huh?"

"You sound funny. I said is anything the matter?"

"Who is this?"

"Van Spanckeren. Tod Van Spanckeren—"

"Oh, yeah." Charlie was fully awake on that. "Sorry, didn't get much sleep last night. Groggy. What can I do for you?"

"Howard Stacey, the museum director—"

Excitedly, Charlie asked, "What about him?"

"He's going fast. You'd better hurry. He's asking for you."

"What the hell are you talking about?"

"You know where he lives in Carefree! The Cave Creek Road?"

"Yes, yes, but what's happened?"

"Scorpion sting. Bad. The doctor is with him. On second thought, you won't have time to make it from where you are. Head for the hospital. Memorial Hospital. South Fifth Avenue."

"In Carefree?"

"Hell, no—*Phoenix*. If you start out right away you'll be there when the ambulance pulls in."

"I'm heading out." He slammed the receiver down, leapt from the bed in one jump and reached for his trousers on the back of a cushy chair.

Shoeless and shirtless, he hurried to the door, opened it and bellowed for Dolly. She swam to the edge of the pool, caught his wave of the arm as a signal, and climbed from the water. She hurriedly grabbed her robe on her way to see what had happened.

"What is it? I thought you were sleeping."

"Howard Stacey's dying!"

He grabbed his wife by her slender wrist and pulled her into the cabana.

"Get dressed. We're heading into town. Memorial Hospital."

She didn't wait for further explanation.

Five minutes later they were taking the steps of the terrace staircase, two at a time.

They sped into town, hoping they wouldn't be caught by a motor patrol. Luck was with them. Conversation was sparse, consisting of one brief exchange of dialogue.

"Scorpion poisoning, sounds horrible."

"From the way Van Spanckeren was talking, also fatal."

"Where was he, outside or inside?"

"Don't know."

"He asked for you? Wonder why?"

"If you let me concentrate on getting there, we'll find out."

They found the hospital after some difficulty due to some confusion with a sign indicator. The ambulance had arrived minutes before. Van Spanckeren was in the lobby of Emergency Section.

"Made that in record time, Charles."

"How is he?"

"Anybody's guess. I followed the ambulance out. The doctor rode with him."

"Poison, huh?"

"Trouble is we don't know how long the poison's been in him. His arm's swollen twice its normal size. They have the anti-toxin here. *This big—*" He made a descriptive gesture with his hand to indicate the condition of the infected arm.

Van Spanckeren spoke to the nurse behind the reception desk. "Any idea how long it'd be before there's some word?"

Hers was an empty face and her shake of the head to signify she didn't know fitted it admirably.

Van Spanckeren made a sign of irritation, but the receptionist didn't catch it.

"You understand, don't you, that this is a police matter?"

The receptionist looked from some files and nodded that she did.

Defeated, Tod suggested they sit in the waiting room, while he went to find the doctor.

Fifteen minutes later, Tod Van Spanckeren returned.

"The doctor thinks he got him in time. The treatment is painful as hell, but the doc says he has to go through it. Like rabies, I guess."

"Can I come along?" said Dolly, springing to her feet.

"Better stay here, Dolly."

"But, Charlie—"

"Here," he insisted.

Dutifully Dolly sat again and picked over some worn magazines.

The two men walked down the long corridor, passing the white-robed doctors, nurses and interns.

"How did you get there so fast?"

"Where, Charles?"

"Stacey's studio."

"I was in a patrol car with a couple of rookies when the call came in. I caught the name, was close, and rode out there fast. Was there inside of ten minutes."

"Means Stacey had the poison in his system for ten minutes plus. At minimum."

Van Spanckeren slowed his gait. "I suppose that's right."

"No way of telling how long it was before he got to the phone."

"Right, again," said the detective. "Why he wants to see you is something you're going to have to discover for yourself. Any ideas?"

"Not a one."

"You'll remember what I said?"

"About what?"

"Letting me know if anything unusual turned up."

"As a matter of fact something has. Coincidence. I was going to call you some time today."

They were approaching the room occupied by Howard Stacey. A doctor was outside talking with a nurse.

Van Spanckeren said, "Doctor, this is Charles Underwood. The man Mr. Stacey asked for."

"Ah, yes. I live close to Howard. If I hadn't been able to get there when I did. Well—well, I did. That's the important thing. Go in. A few minutes, no more. He's rational. In pain. Don't excite him."

Van Spanckeren started to follow Charlie.

"Only one," the doctor said. "One at a time."

The police detective stepped back.

The door closed behind Charlie with a snapping noise. The room was dimly lit, but Howard was clearly visible on the stiff whiteness of the bed things. Charlie came in noiselessly and spoke in a whisper.

"How you feelin', Howard?"

A deadly pale face turned toward the speaker. The museum director looked wretched, drawn and uncomfortable.

"Charlie, thank you for coming to my studio—"

"This isn't—"

"What?"

"This is the hospital, Howard. You're at Memorial Hospital. In Phoenix. You wanted to tell me something?"

Howard tried to lift himself on an elbow, but Charlie gently coaxed him down.

"Yes, yes," Howard gurgled. "I'm getting confused. Like old lady Crowley. Not the police?"

"Tod Van Spanckeren's outside. Do you want to see him?"

The look in Stacey's eyes was fearful. He shook his head.

"No." It was difficult for the man to speak. His mouth tasted like cotton and the words were hard to form.

"The scorpion was in my jar."

"Jar?"

"I keep dead scorpions for—for—"

Charlie thought of "stuffing," but substituted "taxidermy?"

Howard indicated that this was correct.

"Make—interesting—exhibits—so little—unusual—"

"Perhaps you'd better rest, Howard. I can return tomorrow."

"*No.*" Howard was frightened.

"Go on—with what you were saying."

"In the jar—the jar—"

"Yes, in the jar—"

"They're all dead. Been dead for months. But the one—the one that stung me was alive—young. I never saw him before—never. Charlie, no publicity ... Bad for the—museum. Someone put a live scorpion in my jar and when I tipped them out—it—it used its stinger ... someone is trying to murder me. Not the police—you, Charlie, *you* help me. Protect the mu—museum."

He fell into a coma-like state and Charlie left the room to inform the doctor, who hurried in to see his patient.

"Anything interesting, Underwood?"

"Nothing too interesting, but there are a few things I think you should know."

"Begin."

They were walking down the length of the corridor heading back to the waiting room.

"In the morning. What time is good for you?"

"How's ten?"

"Fine. I'll be in your office."

The officer bade goodbye to the Underwoods and left with a uniformed policeman.

Dolly said, "Charlie, I think you could do with a drink."

"Know something?"

"What?"

"I think you're absolutely right."

Arm in arm, they went through the swinging door and greeted the strong sunlight.

Chapter Nine

Tod Van Spanckeren looked younger than forty-five years and the silver-grayness of his hair detracted not at all from this impression. Charlie tried to pick out the flaw in the detective's appearance. Perhaps it was the stylish striped shirts he fancied. The first time Charlie had visited him at the station, Van Spanckeren had worn a thin penciled blue shirt with a narrow dark tie. Not dandyish at all. In mode. Today the stripes were bold and red.

Once again, the policeman was at the window taking note of the street activity below.

"I'll ask my question again. Are you working for someone?"

Charlie shifted his weight uneasily in his chair.

"An interesting question. Brings up several aspects."

"Oh?"

"To answer your question—no, I am not employed by any one individual."

"Good, because—"

Charlie held up his hand in protestation. "Let me finish."

The police official had been toying with the sash of a Venetian blind. He stopped.

"Although I've not, as yet, received any actual payment, several people—three to be exact—have asked my assistance. I never consid-

ered myself officially employed until I've cashed a prospective employer's retainer."

"These three—the names—are they secret?"

Charlie feigned interest in his fingernails.

"Each of the three people is violently opposed to publicity of any
kind. I think that's why they've turned to me instead of the police."

"Go on."

"The first person to seek me out was Lisa Lynch. You know her?"

"I know who she is."

"She was afraid someone was terrorizing her fiancé."

"*Terrorizing?*"

"Phone calls of a threatening nature."

Charlie made no mention of the 'Snow White' aspect.

"Not much to go on," Charlie hedged, "but I promised I'd see what
I could do. Next came a request from Gina Langley's mother—"

"Mrs. Crowley?"

Charlie smiled. "If that's her mother. Same deal—someone was
getting nasty with Gina on the phone."

"Same guy?"

"Guy?"

"Okay—guy or girl—same person?"

"Apparently. Anyway, with Lisa it was a question of helping a
friend with a sticky problem. Old lady Crowley, batty and wild, forgot to sign her check. My retainer. As for Carter—"

The policeman turned sharply from the window.

"Aubery?"

"Carter Aubery, yes."

Van Spanckeren slammed his fist hard on the desk.

"Damn!"

Charlie said nothing, watching the detective's anger.

"Forget that outburst. That museum beat is mine. Understand?"
He spoke rather calmly, considering.

"No."

"I'll explain when you're through. Go ahead. Forget my skinned knuckles."

"Same old sweet song. Carter mentioned a nice figure but I told him I'd sleep on the subject. See what I meant when I said I was technically working for no one?"

Tod Van Spanckeren threw himself into his swivel chair. He ran his hand through his hair.

"You know, Underwood, sometimes it can be damned discouraging. No slur on you."

"I'm in the dark."

"Why people don't trust the police. All this hush-hush. They know me. I know them. Why couldn't they have come to me if they were getting these threatening calls?"

"I've already told you—fear of publicity."

"What the hell did they think I was going to do—sell their woes to the papers?" He picked up a pencil and brandished it threateningly in Charlie's direction.

"Are you telling me everything you know?"

"Ordinarily I wouldn't have told you this much, but I discovered something at the Ullman farewell that changes the complexion of the whole thing."

"In what way?"

"I think I can prove to you how Ullman was—murdered."

Van Spanckeren's eyes gave the impression of being dazed, then of shrinking. His mouth seemed to enlarge.

"You can prove what you're saying? Actually prove it?"

Charlie looked at his watch. The time was close to eleven.

"The museum's been open for an hour. We'll have to go there."

"I'll get a squad car."

"No," said Charlie, "no need for that. I'll see that you get back in time."

"In time? In time for *what*?"

"Your routine."

"Buddy, that *museum* is my routine. You drive your own bus. I'll get a squad car. Meet you there."

From Police Headquarters to the Langley Memorial Museum was a distance of approximately nine miles. Charlie made good time, encountered almost no traffic. The squad car was there before him.

A Lady Booster dressed in black, with a grotesque corsage that threatened to engulf her chin, greeted him.

"The guest book. Please sign it."

"Later," snapped Charles as he hurried by her.

"Well— "

"Said the thirsty man on the desert."

The police detective and a uniformed policeman were standing at the spot Ullman took leave of life.

"Van Spanckeren said something to the man in uniform and the man stepped back from the scene.

Charlie looked about him. The museum was deserted with the exception of the investigators, the Lady Booster, and a trio of withered, seedy crones. Charlie noticed something else. The Rodins were missing, as was much of the opening exhibition. The walls were spotted with gaps broken by an occasional nondescript work.

"Hey, what happened?"

"Don't ask *me*. Guess this is the in-between day."

"The Rodins and the other things? Where are they?"

"I don't know. About Henry Ullman—"

"Not as easy as I thought. No Rodin. But I can improvise, reconstruct the scene. The mob, where Ullman was seated—"

Charlie went over the entire thing, excused himself, went around to the other side of the wall partition, found the stick used for opening vents and reconstructed what he thought to be the enactment of a murder.

"Grand Slam!" he shouted, as the pole racked through to touch the pedestal.

In the far end of the room, the Lady Booster soured.

"*Sssh*!" she hissed. "Respect for others!"

The three harpies were seated, side by side, eating tangerines on a marble bench.

When Charlie returned to Van Spanckeren's side of the partition, the detective's expression was impossible to decipher.

Glumly, Tod said: "Won't hold water, Underwood. Not a drop. This is guesswork. Pure guesswork. Motive? Where the hell is the motive?"

"I don't have the answer to that."

"I—I—"

"Come on, Tod, why the stall?"

"I admit it's probable."

"What's the reservation?"

"Not good enough to warrant an investigation."

"You don't want an investigation."

"I admit it. I told you this was my museum, my beat and it is. Don't get me wrong. The minute you can hand me something solid, I spring. But this is not good enough."

Charlie sat beside him, puzzled.

Van Spanckeren looked at the uniformed patrolman uneasily. To Charlie he said in a *sub rosa* tone, "Don't misunderstand. Try to get the picture."

"I'll try if you paint it."

"You know much about India?"

"India?"

"Do you?"

"No."

"Neither do I, but from what I've read I understand they—the Indians—look upon screwballs—er—people who are—what the Irish call 'touched'—"

"*Touched*?"

"Would you mind shutting up until I get this out?"

Charlie silenced himself.

"You didn't know Langley. The husband."

Charlie wanted to say no, he didn't, but he bit his lip.

"He was the last of the Langleys. Osbert. Phoenix has only been what you could call a city for the last quarter of a century, but the Langleys—they go back to the Civil War days. Right here in this territory. The Langleys are part of the Phoenix legend. Half the schools, hospitals, libraries—you name it—in this state are named after Langleys. Like I say—part of the legend of the West."

He made a gesture that took in the room, "This museum." He was cognizant of the empty spaces on the walls and looked troubled.

"Mrs. Langley is always mixed in with some charity. Take Carter Aubery. Owns considerable stock in every newspaper in town. Publishes his own magazine. These are people who—"

Charlie broke his promise, "Sacred cows?"

"I don't like to put it in exactly that perspective. Oh, I know they're getting old. Getting foolish, but the point is—they do represent something and if they're shown as murderers or idiots—well—it would be embarrassing, to say the least. All I try to do is keep them out of trouble, but if there was anything totally illegal, I'd have no choice but to take action. Understand?"

Before Tod Van Spanckeren could say anything further, Charlie was asking, "And Dorothea Darnell? You mean to tell me you know these people so intimately that Gina Langley's secretary, a member of the board, was unknown to you?"

"Okay, I lied. I checked on you. Someone said—"

"Someone? *Who?*"

"Mike Jarvits. He said you were going to be here for a week or so, no longer. I figure you'd be heading back East soon and this would have no meaning for you. If I told you about her you might have stayed."

"I'm staying. So what's with Darnell?"

"Dorothea. Mind you, Charles, this was a rare dish. If you liked the type."

"The type doesn't sound too appealing."

"How do you mean?"

"Looked like 'Snow White,' didn't she?"

"Snow White who?"

"Skip it. I referred to her pasty skin and black hair."

"Oh, yeah, she was arty, but a mean one. I had quite a dossier on that *chica*."

"Chica?"

"Spanish."

"For chick?"

"No, for *girl*. Her specialty was giving her charms freely. Keeping notes. Tape recordings. The works. When you first met her none of this was evident. Smooth. Oh, so smooth. Never have found out how Gina Langley connected with her. This gal was clever. Exceptionally so. I was never able to find out who exactly she was blackmailing." Charlie said nothing about Carter Aubery.

"L.A. police have an ugly file on her. Nothing but the top material—producers, foreign diplomats—no convictions. No one would testify. I tried my damndest to get rid of her. Threatened her with exposure."

"No dice."

"She would look at me with those eyes. Those dark eyes and say, 'Are you accusing *Gina Langley's* secretary of these things? What ever will the papers say?'" He gritted his teeth. "Naturally I had no choice but to give her enough rope and hope she'd hang herself. She's gone. Maybe she did that very thing."

"Or someone did it for her."

"There's always that possibility."

Again, Charlie thought of mentioning the message of the phone calls, but he decided against it, substituting instead, "Then my idea about Ullman has no merit?"

"I didn't say it didn't have merit. I say only that it's far-fetched."

"Have you carried on any investigation about Snow—sorry—Dorothea Darnell?"

"Has someone reported her missing?"

Charlie decided on a new line of attack.

"Have you heard anything regarding Howard Stacey?"

"He'll be fine, according to the doctor. Sick, but nothing fatal. They plan to let him go. I talked to him. No complaints."

The Lady Booster was winging in their direction.

"Which is Mr. Charles Underwood?"

"Huh?"

"Underwood. Charles Underwood. Like the typewriter."

"That's me," said Charlie.

"A telephone message. In Mr. Stacey's and Mr. Jarvits' office."

To Tod, Charlie said, "Must be Dolly. She knows I'm here."

He walked to the phone, picked up the receiver.

"Hello, darling," came her cheery voice. "Your wife."

"I gathered as much."

"I'm at Lisa's. We're having coffee. Can you come by for me? These Phoenix taxis charge so much."

"Be there in an hour."

"Good. We can have lunch on our way out to Lars'. After you left this morning, he called and invited us out to see some new works. I accepted."

"I'm glad you did. Anything with Lisa?"

"Yes, I'm confident the paintings will be a treat, too."

"Huh?"

"Yes, darling, I know you're anxious to see them."

"Can't talk?"

"Clever boy."

"Be there within the hour."

Tod Van Spanckeren was in the office.

"To clarify—" stated the police officer. "You are working for no *one* individual?"

"In the sense I've received no retainers. You won't buy my theory on Ullman's murder?"

"Not from what you've shown me. Besides, as I've told you, I want a motive. Give me a motive. If a nut is going to indiscriminately murder someone, he doesn't plan something of this nature. Too contrived."

Van Spanckeren doubled his fist, brought it to his mouth and performed a fake cough.

"Uh—Charlie boy—you've met the museum crowd now. Tell me—er—has the subject of—drugs ever been mentioned?"

"*Drugs?*"

"Narcotics?"

"No."

"Well, I'll be in touch."

The two men shook hands. The policeman, followed by the driver of the squad car, left the museum, leaving a very perturbed gentleman from New Hampshire face to face with a Lady Booster dragon.

Charlie left a moment later.

"I hate Pancho Villa's Villa," exclaimed Lisa. "And I think it's horrid of you to continually mention Dorothea."

Dolly crossed her lovely legs.

"But you did know her?"

"For a short time. Woman looked like a nun. Holier than thou. Eyes cast down. Sweet. Like some poisons."

Both women had been sitting on the sofa. Dolly rose and took a few steps toward the window.

"I hate to mention this, Lisa, and perhaps Charlie would object, but don't forget it was you who came to *us* for help."

"I know."

"Then, baby, you've got to tell us everything you know, or suspect."

Lisa unfolded the piece of linen.

"You're right. I've been behaving atrociously. No excuse. Yes, Mike knew her. I never knew they were more than friendly—until—"

"Until *what?*"

"After she disappeared. A week or so. I casually mentioned her name and he blew into a rage. Told me never to mention her name in his presence. She was gone. I was to forget her."

"*Gone?*"

"From Phoenix. I suppose that's what he meant."

A not-so-convinced Dolly replied, "I imagine so."

"He was looking forward to this position so much. So very much. Everything was going to be wonderful. But last night—last night—he said it might be wiser if we returned to New York. That's what he's planning to do. He's going to tell Howard. Dolly, he'll never get the chance he has here. Take years. He doesn't seem to care. Get away, that's all he thinks about."

"How did they happen to meet? Tell Dolly the truth."

"You mean Dorothea and Michael?"

"No—Gina Langley."

"Mike—Mike was working at the Whitney. Gina breezed in one day. Chatted. He didn't think anything of it. Next day, she asked him out to lunch. When the Whitney director found out it was Gina Langley making the request, he practically ordered Mike to accept the invitation. After that, nature took its course."

"You're not suggesting—"

"No, of course, I'm not. I know Gina. That whole thing was her way, nothing more. Why has everything changed? I keep asking myself that."

"That's what you want Charlie to find out, isn't it?"

"If he can."

"He can. Then, you think the idea of Mike and Dorothea carrying on some kind of affair is nonsense."

"I don't know—I said I never heard the name when you first asked, because I was so embarrassed, I suppose. Angry."

The radio was on. Dolly recognized a tune.

"Lisa," she gushed. "The radio—turn it up."

She did. Lisa, too, recognized the tune.

"Isn't that—'Girl of All Nations'?"

"From *Bring 'Em Back Alive*, yes. You played the stripper."

"And you were the flower girl. Oh, I remember. That show opened and closed faster than a Venus Fly Trap."

Dolly seized her friends' hand. The radio blared. They sang and danced in an attempt to capture a memory:

> "Girl of all nations,
> I love you so.
> Your intoxicating feathers
> Thrill me so.
> Can this be love?"

It was thus, heels kicking, smiles professional, Charles Underwood found his life's companion, and companion's old sidekick awaiting his arrival.

Lunch was a disappointment. The tea room had boastfully proclaimed by way of a sign, that it served the best French cuisine on the desert. The sign lied. The omelet was underdone, the wine of the establishment inclined towards sourness, the service wretched.

"I hope," said a dejected Charlie, "Lars Waddington's paintings will not be as bad as this." He poked at a salad with a fork.

"Poor beast. Beauty knows how you dislike a bad meal."

"Not at all, but when a joint says its food is the best, it should, at least, be fairly decent."

"A few things have been established," she said, anxious to change the subject. "From what you've told me, it's a safe bet Tod Van Spanckeren's job is to cover up for the museum's board of directors. And the mention of narcotics. What does that denote?"

"Can't say. Carter mentioned something about a drug. When I called him on it, he clammed shut."

Dolly bit into an onion roll.

"We do know that Dorothea and Lisa had some liaison, and I believe that's what caused Lisa to be so emotional. Jealousy."

"From all I can gather, this Dorothea—"

"*Snow White.*"

"Okay, Snow White. In any case, she was in very bad odor. She appears to be the original Fanny Hill, pen in hand—"

"Charlie, you say that Tod wasn't at all receptive to your theory about Ullman's murder."

"Not in the slightest. Can't figure him out. He keeps pumping me for information. I sensed a grudging affection for Dorothea even though he admitted she was a rat. Fits in."

Dolly had no trouble with her appetite. She fished what remained of Charlie's salad onto her plate.

"What fits in?"

"The first time I met Tod. At his office. He mentioned Rumpelstiltskin in describing Hank Ullman. That mean anything to you—Rumpelstiltskin?"

Dolly swallowed hard. "Wasn't he the awful little gentleman who thumped on some floor so hard he fell through?"

"Yeah. I think that's about it. Not too important. What *is* important is that Gina once said Dorothea had difficulty separating life from *The Book of Grimm's*, giving people pet fairy-tale names."

"I recall."

"I've known many a police detective and somehow—*Rumpelstiltskin*—it doesn't sound like a cop speaking."

"You think Dorothea and Tod were seeing something of each other?"

"*¿Quién sabe?*"

"What dear?"

"*¿Quién sabe?*"

"What does it mean?"

"Wipe your luscious face and get a move on."

The ride to Lars' studio was brief. Ten minutes or so. The house resembled a jacal, a structure of branches and ocotillo spines. This was its appearance as you approached along the dusty, unpaved road. Actually, the main part of the house was low to the back. The ramada, that portion of the patio roof that jetted out, was entirely of branches and sticks, but the house, hardly more than one large room, was built of adobe brick.

Lars came to the door on Charlie's "Hello, anybody home?" He leaned heavily on his cane, smiling, and a fat Siamese cat walked in between his master's legs in a dance-like prance.

"Come right in, you young people," Lars said happily as he opened the screen door.

"*Meow!*"

"This is Fat Cat," explained the painter. "Friend of mine was a jazzist and found Fat Cat foraging in some ashcan. When he brought pussy to me, he was not much in the way of looks. Eyes half-closed. Mangy, fur matted. First few nights he was here he ran wild on the desert. What a racket."

Dolly leaned down to stroke Fat Cat's coat.

"Why, he's gorgeous!" she gushed. "You did wonders for him."

Lars suppressed a chuckle.

"I took him to the vet. That quickly took care of his most pressing problems; now he's quite content to eat, sleep and be petted. A good life. Not like a cat, ordinary house cat, more like a dog. Did you notice how he came to the door? A throwback. They used to guard palace gates."

"Really?" said Dolly as she and Charlie followed Lars' slow steps to that section of the room stocked with easels, canvases and frames.

"That crook in his tail is a throwback, too. Court ladies, when they bathed, put their rings on kitty's tail. The bend in the tail made loss of the jewelry unlikely."

"Imagine."

"Haven't come here for a lecture on fur people, have you?"

"I adore Siamese. Charlie does too, but he'll never admit it."

"More of a beagle man myself," Charlie said in way of defense.

There was a sofa covered by a Mexican serape near the easel, set close to a panel of sliding doors that led onto the desert terrain.

"Usually, I begin to paint early. This spot is good for north light."

The Underwoods observed a score of paintings scattered about.

"You certainly manage to produce," said Charlie, appreciating the man's drive.

Lars looked at his hands. They were slightly twisted, the fingers stiff. He ran one hand over the other, as if he were washing them.

"Won't be able to do many more, I fear. These you see here purchased long ago. I must return them to their owners. My need for customers has always made it difficult to secure enough works for a showing."

Fat Cat leaped into Charlie's lap.

"I notice that most of the paintings at the Langley Museum are now gone."

Waddington gestured at the paintings scattered around the floor.

"Why, yes. These don't belong to the museum. I've donated three, however. I couldn't do any less. I owed it to Gina."

"But the Rodin castings? There was a Rembrandt, too. I saw it. And a Darrel Austin, and a Pollock—what's become of them?"

"Their owners took them back. They lent them to Gina for the opening days."

The Underwoods were at sea and Lars knew it. He intended to explain, but paused before asking Dolly to open the cigarette box which was next to an overflowing copper ashtray. A few butts soiled the floor around the easel, too.

"Here you are," she said, holding out the box, wooden with a painting of an Italian street scene on the lid.

"I smoke too much."

Charlie fished for his lighter.

"No, thank you, Charlie. With arthritis it's good to keep going. A small thing like lighting my own cigarette is good for my ego and I pretend it passes for exercise." He laughed kindly. "I loathe exercise. Always have."

He took a deep puff and sighed happily.

"I suppose I could be classified as a tobaccic."

"Interesting classification," Charlie replied, stroking Fat Cat who had taken a fancy to him.

"I suppose a love of tobacco, excessive love—like anything else—could pass for addiction. Or is that a poor word to employ?"

"I've never given it much thought."

"We don't consider it criminal to become addicted to tobacco—that's why I think people rarely think about it as addiction. Yet take morphine—"

The artist was taking the long way around, but he was edging close to a point he considered important.

"Morphine?"

"A drug that many people throughout history have used. If a person has access to it he can live a productive life and no one's the wiser. However, if caught, he's a criminal and sent to prison. Alcohol, on the other hand, enjoys a special kind of license. I imagine this is because it carries its own machine for remorse."

Charlie and Dolly stared silently at the man who sat on a high wooden stool and spoke like a pundit.

"To the paintings. Gina got the idea for the museum and everyone loves Gina. But her personality and attitude toward existence and life is—how shall we put it—*theatrical*? When she gets an idea most everyone tries to go along with it, because she has done so very much for this town and her husband, too, when he was alive. Her last husband, that is. Osbert Langley.

"She's not practical. Hank Ullman, bless him with all his faults, knew that the museum was nonsense. The city has been planning one for a long, long time, carefully and sensibly. He never said anything to Gina, understand, but he got the city to put the land at her—disposal—in the hopes she'd eventually turn the whole thing over to the city, heavily endowed. Even Carter's designs—his architects—kept one eye on the future of the city. Mind you, the building was financed by Gina, the whole thing, but she loses interest—fast. Everyone donated works for the opening to please her, but everyone wanted them back. Poor Gina. She didn't realize a museum is only as good as its collection."

"Why doesn't she use her own collection? A superb one."

Lars laughed, not unkindly. "That's what I mean about Gina. We might be inclined to see her as bizarre, foolish, if you will, yet she's smart enough to keep those works for her own pleasure. Carter, too."

"What happens then? With the museum?"

"City can't take it over yet. Not until Gina signs it away. Naturally, there's no sense in attempting to pretend the museum will stay open. It's been the whipping boy of the art world. Laughable. I can exhibit. Carter would be amenable to showing his collection, for a time. But that's a huge place to fill with works. That's rough for Michael Jarvits."

"In what way?"

"Gina plans to appoint him director of her museum. That's why she got him here. But there really is no museum, or there won't be shortly."

"And if the city takes it over?"

"I imagine Mr. Jarvits could stay on as an assistant, but I doubt it. The city doesn't offer the money a woman like Gina Langley does."

Dolly asked, "Lars, this may sound naïve, but seriously—what makes a museum outstanding? Its management?"

"Its *collection*, Dolly. What I was saying a moment ago. What it has in its *permanent* collection. That, I would say, more than anything else. Traveling exhibits and all of that are admirable, but they can be had by any reputable museum. Yes—the permanent collection, that's the thing."

Quickly, he changed mood.

"Anything new about Howard Stacey?"

"He'll be home in a day or so."

"I must call and see if I can help. He doesn't have anyone with him at his studio. Alone. Scorpion poisoning. That meant death at one time. A sting like that will kill young children. Several deaths like that every year here in the Valley. Stay away from date palms, Dolly."

"Date palms?"

"In the trunk leaves of the date trees—scorpions often live there."

"I'll never eat another date."

"My new works. Just four. I thought you'd like to see them. You'll be the first."

Dolly said, "We're honored."

The painting on the easel had been partially covered by a white cloth. Lars drew it back. The work displayed Waddington's expected skill, individual approach and technical proficiency.

"I call it *Welcome to the Casa*."

In the background, the work showed a house of Spanish Colonial inspiration, but it was unearthly, vague. The foreground was a patio, enclosed on all sides by bird cages. A circular table drew attention. Four people were seated, three women and one man. By the first woman working counter-clockwise, sat an Ibizan hound. The woman's body was trim, her Spanish costume clinging to her body. The woman next to her was gowned in a ridiculous Chinese outfit; the man beside her was wrapped in a printer's apron. The fourth figure at the table had flesh the color of paste and long, black hair. At her side, ugly and cruel, squatted a repulsive dwarf.

Charlie easily could have named the figures. They were obvious. Over the head of each, Lars had painted a brightly colored paper bag. That is, for the females. The bag over the printer's head was mortician gray.

Charlie put Fat Cat on the floor, stood and stepped to the easel. Pointing to the first figure he said, "Gina?"

Lars made no comment.

Charlie's finger moved to the second chair, the woman in Chinese garments. "Mrs. Crowley." Next to the printer, "Carter Aubery." Then the last: Snow White?"

"I prefer to let my paintings speak for themselves."

"What does it mean?"

"At the opening of the museum, you asked me that question. Do you recall, Dolly?"

Fat Cat had transferred his affection to Dolly and rested comfortably in her lap.

"I'm afraid I don't recall, Lars."

"You asked me to explain a painting. What it meant."

"I do recall something now. You said—if you could explain it you wouldn't have to paint it."

"Excellent memory."

"Thanks."

Charlie, still looking at the painting, asked, "This Snow White—Dorothea Darnell—did you know her well?"

Lars took some time before answering, "She was an odd child. I doubt if anyone even knew her. Herself included."

"Why do you say that?"

"Riddled with neuroses, a depressive. Trustworthy one instant, avaricious the next. She had the capacity for making people like her, then she would turn—I—well, I have no desire to speak disrespectfully of—"

He broke off in mid-thought. Dolly ceased stroking the cat.

"Forgive me," he said.

"No, no," insisted Charlie. "You were about to say—?"

"I was about to say that you haven't seen the other three. *Casa* is but one."

This was an ineffectual attempt to cover his slip. He realized this as well as the Underwoods.

"I liked her at first. Seemed childlike and innocent. Yes, innocent is the word. She often came here for a glass of wine. Dorothea liked to drink sherry and munch vanilla wafers. I thought she was an angel. A gamine. So appealing. That was one side of Dorothea—"

"And the other--?"

Lars' hand, the one which held the cigarette, began to shake.

Charlie said, "When was the last time you saw her? Do you recall?"

"Yes, she came out here one morning and told me I'd have to see her that night. At Gina's. I drove to the house about ten, I'd say. May have been later. But not much later. There'd been an accident at the house."

"Accident?"

"One of Gina's dogs—" He looked at the painting, singling out the Ibizan by the chair with a nod of the head. "Lorca. Named for the Spanish playwright. A car had hit Lorca." He paused before continuing. "I remember thinking as I drove along that stretch of road from the gate to the house, and my car picked out the hearse, that something terrible had happened. I thought it was Mrs. Crowley. I thought she had died and was riding to the funeral parlor. She's so old. Always falling down, or swallowing the wrong thing, but she's a warhorse. Confused, but still a warhorse. Hope I can retain a fraction of that pep when I'm her age. Oh, yes, believe it or not, Gina's mother is much older than I."

Dolly made an attempt to smile.

Charlie's voice was professional and calm.

"What hearse?"

"A van from the pet cemetery. They were taking the poor animal to the crematorium."

"Was anyone else at the house?"

Lars pretended he hadn't heard.

"Was anyone—else--?"

"I—no—that is—"

"Who else was there?" There was something of a military strength in the way Charlie asked the question. Lars responded accordingly.

"I don't want to get anyone in—"

"Lars," said Charlie sympathetically, "this is all 'off the cuff.' I'm here to look at some paintings."

"Thank you," said Lars and he appeared to believe this. "I think I saw Mike Jarvits' car. A Volkswagen."

"But no Mike?"

Silence.

"*But no Mike?*" repeated Charlie.

"The driver in the van from the pet cemetery—"

Dolly clutched the fur at the back of Fat Cat's neck, saying as she did so, "He wasn't Mike?"

"Oh, no, I saw the driver clearly. Young chap, much younger than Mike Jarvits. Blond. But there was someone sitting beside him and when the van drove by—I had to pull over to the side—my reflexes aren't all they might be, and that van was coming at a rapid clip. The man beside the driver—I got one quick look—but it did look like Mike ducking out of sight, as if he didn't want to be seen. Mark me, Charlie, I can't be positive."

"But his car was there?"

"Looked like his Volkswagen. There are no lights out along that drive. The front of the house has some lamps. They glow, that's all. No illumination otherwise."

"Did you ask about the car?"

"No. Juan, the butler, said Dorothea had left that morning and not returned."

Charlie took out his notebook and jotted these things down.

"One thing more, Lars."

"Yes?"

"Dorothea and Mike—did they ever express interest in each other, I mean above and beyond ordinary appearances?"

"Not that I know of."

"Never any gossip about them?"

"I've heard none, and I'm always hearing this or that, usually it's nonsense. I never heard anything of that sort about Michael and Snow—excuse me—*Dorothea*."

Charlie had no more questions, and he and Dolly followed Lars to the door. He insisted on showing them out. Exercise, he said. Fat Cat trailed behind.

"I enjoyed that painting, Lars. And your discussion of addiction. To tobacco."

"There are many worse things in life, aren't there?"

"Oh," said Dolly, "Charlie's named everyone in the painting but the dwarf and the dog. Does he have a name, Lars?"

"I've given the dog no name."

They were at the screen door. Fat Cat crawled up the thin wire-work, his swinging tail making him appear almost monkey-like.

"They called them monkey-cats when they first brought them into the country."

"He looks like one."

"Down, Fat Cat," said Lars and he brushed at the animal with the back of his hand. The cat, with a petulant meow, jumped back to the floor. "But," said Lars pleasantly, "I must confess I have thought of a name for the dwarf. I call him 'Rumpelstiltskin.'"

At the car, Dolly felt an odd sensation of being watched. Swiftly she looked back. Only then did she realize that the trees in the yard were potentially hostile.

There were four trees in all. Large, overgrown, and neglected. Even the dates the trees bore, shriveled and black, appeared threatening.

A dry wind drifted in her direction.

Chapter Ten

The moon was up, the stars were out.

Dolly stood at the door of the cabana enjoying the hypnotic grandeur of the deepening night. Lighted candles, flickering and ghostly, floated on wooden pads in the pool. They looked like scores of tiny boats setting off on long journeys, each hosting a Marco Polo.

From one of the cabanas came the sound of music. Inwardly she felt that things were to be all right in time, and for some reason, inexplicable at the moment, the music was part of this sensation.

Charlie, in slacks and opened sport shirt, was writing at the desk. For him, things were beginning to fall into place. Still too many loose ends to declare that he was getting anywhere, but, nonetheless, he was confident that he was heading in the right direction.

He was employing the Underwood Induction-Deduction system, a device of his own making. More a method of clarification than anything else, it occasionally produced something significant.

On file cards he had written a word or phrase that somehow fit in with the shenanigans he found whirling about in the Valley of the Sun.

On card #1 he had written:

#1 DOROTHEA — WHAT DOES SHE HAVE ON THEM?
WHERE IS SHE?

#2 DRUG TODD VAN SPANCKEREN

LARS WADDINGTON

CARTER AUBERY

#3 MORMONS

DEATH OF LORCA

(LDS)

#4 <u>BOARD</u>

SNOW WHITE (?)

ULLMAN (X)

HOWARD (X)

CARTER AUBERY

MRS. CROWLEY

GINA

#5 INFORMANT/CALLER

CARTER AUBERY

Dolly turned from the night and faced her husband, watching him as he went about his task. His concentration fascinated her.

"Now," gushed Charlie in anticipation, "we can begin!"

"Can I help?"

"'Course you can. You know I consider the female mind far superior to the male when it comes to matters analytical."

Dolly beamed and came to the desk. Charlie pulled out a low chair and Dolly sat close to her husband. He held the first card in his right hand.

"This is on Dorothea. Snow White. I've two questions here."

Dolly took the card and read what was written.

"*What does she have on them?* Easy – blackmail."

"Everything points in that direction. I don't think there's any doubt. Question is, what does she have that ties it all together?"

"Some conspiracy? They were all in it together—whatever *it* is.

Dorothea found out and went in for some extortion."

"No, I think not. The group idea. Listening to Lars this afternoon, I got the impression Dorothea somehow worked on each of them in a different way. With Lars she was a child. Tod described her as a sexpot and so it goes. A chameleon. She got something on each of them, in her own way. Every man has his private skeleton or two."

"Or three."

"Or more. Anyway, Dorothea managed to rattle a few bones. Next question?"

Dolly read the card's second inquiry: *"Where is she?"*

"She might have been paid off. Given money and told to get out of town before the sun sets—real Old West stuff. But, I don't buy this theory. One reason being that appointment she made with Lars. Obviously, he was to show at the house with cash."

Dolly crossed her long, slender legs.

"What makes you so positive?"

"The way Lars put it this afternoon. Recall—he said: 'She told me I'd have to see her that night.' *Have to.* That girl wasn't asking him to come to the house, she was ordering him to. Blackmail. Carter Aubery's admission of the same substantiates this. The mysterious caller asks an interesting question; the important word being *buried.* I'd say someone, person or persons unknown, knocked off dear Snow White and hid the body. She died, I believe, some time between that hour she left Lars' place and he drove along Gina's driveway that same night."

"Charlie," said Dolly thoughtfully, "I've been thinking about what Lars said—that van from the pet cemetery—do you suppose—?"

"I think there's a damn good possibility that both Lorca and Snow White were in that van."

"You'll never be able to prove that."

"I think I will."

Dolly's lower jaw drooped and struggled with a single word: "How?"

"Next card." He handed it to her.

"*Drug?*"

"We have Tod V. questioning me on the topic. Lars Waddington with his academic spiel this afternoon, and Carter Aubery tossing off references to the subject—"

"Charlie, I'm on to something. Could that be what Snow White discovered? The museum board is an addicts' academy?"

Professionally he said, "Card three."

She read: "*Mormons—LDS—Death of Lorca*. I can't make any sense of this at all. I don't mean about the dog dying, but this Mormon Church business. Latter-day Saints."

"Okay. Where did we first hear the letters?"

"That's easy—Chinatown Lil—old Mrs. Crowley. She told Gina that if she hadn't been fooling around with the Mormons, Lorca never would have died."

Charlie smiled, leaned over and kissed his wife on her cheek.

"I adore you," he said.

"Then I've solved something?"

"No, dear, but I love you anyway. What Mrs. Crowley mentioned was LDS, yes, but because the Mormon Church is strong in this area we made the error of assuming she spoke the abbreviation for Latter-day Saints. No way to tie that in with drugs. Also, remember that remarkable creature is continually confusing things. One day with another, one person with another—and so on."

"Waddington's talk set me straight. Old Crowley didn't mean LDS at all. What she meant was L.S.D."

"L.S.D.? Isn't that a—a drug?" She answered her own question.

"Right you are. A non-addictive drug. Everything I've read on the topic brings in this creative thing. Apparently it frees some inner-locked ability to see a creative work clearly from inception to completion."

"What you told me about Carter Aubery's painting would fit it. A drug that Gina mentioned."

He sighed as he attempted to work out the mathematical significance of the file cards. He repeated Mrs. Crowley's words, "If you hadn't been fooling around with L.D.S.—"

"The dog never would have died."

"Then what we have to discover is the tie between the drug and the dog's death. Next card"

"But—"

"Next card."

Dolly took it and placed it face up with the others.

"Why, this is nothing more than a list of the board members."

"More than that. Can't you see the marks after the names?"

She looked again.

"After Dorothea's name, 'Snow White,' a question mark ... Mean-ing—"

"Is she dead or alive?"

"After Ullman's name, an X."

"Dead."

"After Howard Stacey's name, another X."

"Someone tried to kill him. Someone who knew he was planning to work with the jar of dead scorpions."

"Other three names have no marks."

"They haven't died, disappeared—or had an attempt made on their lives."

"What about those not on the board? Mike Jarvits, Tod Van—"

Charlie laughed good-naturedly.

"Is that a joke?"

"No, but I was thinking that so far no one but you and I accept the theory Ullman was murdered."

"Hadn't thought of that."

"Nor have an employer to date."

"What about Aubery?"

"I don't think I'm going to be able to turn down his financial of-fer. He, however, believes that everything's aimed at him. Mike is out to get him because Mike was in love with Dorothea, and Mike has the idea Carter somehow managed to get *her* out of the way. That brings up the last card."

Dolly stacked the others and studied the new one.

"Informant?"

"Who told Carter that Mike and Dorothea were lovers? Lars didn't notice anything. And he's one wide-awake gentleman."

"Don't forget the way Lisa behaved. She said Mike hit the ceiling when Dorothea's name came up."

"That doesn't have to mean they were in any way involved emotionally."

"Explain, please."

"What if Mike and someone else did do harm to Dorothea? He'd be just as jumpy at the mention of the name."

"Then why would the informant make Carter think Mike was going to kill *him* for harming Snow White? Wouldn't make sense. And who is this informant?"

"I trust it's the same person's who's been asking about Snow White's resting place."

Dolly pushed the cards away and yawned.

"All very interesting. I am dog tired. Bed for me."

Charlie took the cards and placed them in his shirt pocket.

"Sorry to hear that, dear."

"Why?"

"Because I've got a little business to attend to tonight. I thought you might want to come along."

Dolly was already at the closet, selecting a jacket to wear.

As they drove, the bright moon, round and watching, seemed inconsistent with a sharp chill that crept in from the desert. There was a promise of rain.

"Nights get cold," said Charlie, putting his arm around his wife. She snuggled close to him, her head on his shoulder.

"Charles," she cooed sensually, "I love you, Ch-Ch-Charlie."

He kissed her forehead. She cooed again, but said nothing. She ran her hand over the firmness of his thigh. He kissed her forehead again.

Breathily, she asked, "Where are we going?"

He turned and stared at her lovely face and wide eyes. She returned a lover's gaze.

"The Dreamy Pastures Mortuary."

The Pastures lay half between the town of Tempe, named for its similarity with the Grecian Vale of Tempe, and sprawling South Phoenix. Even from some distance it could be picked out. A gigantic, fluorescent-lighted caricature of a cur, breed unknown, glowed and faded, glowed and faded. The lights of his tails were not functioning. A short circuit.

Absurdly designed to represent a gingerbread house, the mortuary stood in a funereal glade of eucalyptus. They parked, walked down a cobble-stoned path, came to the gingerbread door and knocked.

It was practically no time before it opened and they were face-to-face with a rather sullen young man. He needed a shave, his eyes were bloodshot and his skin transparent. He wasn't an albino, but it was skin approaching that texture and coloring.

"You the copper?"

"Underwood, yes."

Charlie flashed his private investigator's credentials from the licensing board in New Hampshire and snapped the wallet shut swiftly. The attendant barely looked.

"Too bad," said the young man. "I was hoping you'd brought some business. Been slow as hell here all day. One Chihuahua."

"May we come in?" asked Charlie.

"Yeah." He held open the screen door and the Underwoods entered.

"Oh," gushed Dolly, "this is a lovely reception room."

"Ain't it though," snapped the young man, mockingly. "This is where the owners sit, while I make arrangements. You two ain't owners, so come in here. I've got things to do."

Dolly faked a smile and they followed the young man into the adjoining room, a hard white room with silver tubing leading into and from metal ovens in the walls. Aluminum containers, draining boards, bottles of colored liquid. The room stank of disinfectant.

The young man sat behind his desk, working on a wiring connection. Charlie watched without speaking.

"For his tail," said the young man.

"Tail?"

"On the sign. The mutt's tail blew. He supposed to wag it. Y'know—like he's happy to be here."

Dolly faked another smile.

"Unusual. A gingerbread design."

"Yeah. This joint used to be some kind of hot dog stand. The Witch's Inn, I think. Yeah, that was it—The Witch's Inn. The chicks who hopped from car to car dressed like they was old witches, see, only the skirts was cut off in the back, so's that when they turned around you could get a fancy look at their behinds."

Charlie cleared his throat. "I see."

"Took this job to help out this guy and his wife. She's got asthma bad. I was floating, knew they was in this burg, so's when I passed through I give him a buzz and they give me this job. What the hell. You hungry?"

"No, no," said Dolly, a shade too hysterically for comfort.

"I'm gonna have me a bite. What did you want to know again?"

Charlie had explained everything in detail on the phone. The attendant was stalling.

"I understand you take care of Gina Langley's pets."

"The dead ones, yeah. Here at Dreamy Pastures we call 'em Fur People. A gasser, huh?"

He indicated the crematoriums along the walls.

Dolly tried for a third fake smile, but failed.

"Yeah, that Langley dame keeps this place going. Old parrots, parakeets, alley cats, monkeys. No telling what you get when you go out there."

A baloney sandwich on rye and a container of milk stood beside a stiff Chihuahua. The attendant took out his snack, slammed the door leaning against it, and returned to the desk.

He sat and poured some milk from the container into a plastic cup.

"What was the name of that animal?"

"His name was Lorca. An Ibizan Hound. Less than a month ago. Couldn't forget the animal. The breed is extremely rare."

"Oh, that was—that—rare-looking dog."

"With the short legs and the thick head."

"I remember. I told the owners. They had never seen one, either. See, I kinda like this place. Work's easy, and me—I'm trying to buy them out. Y'know, a little at a time? Good town. I like it here."

"Who was it that called you?"

"I know you're a cop, but would you mind telling me what's going on? What's so important about the mutt—I mean—Fur Person?"

"In that neighborhood, residents suspect someone has been poisoning animals. Mrs. Crowley thinks maybe that's what happened to Lorca."

"You mean the old lady?"

"Yes."

"Bat Tower Belle. Don't she remember nothing'? That animal was run over. Hit and run. No poison. He ran into the driveway and got whammed."

"And the driver got away."

The young man had been munching his baloney on rye with indifferent appetite. He held half the sandwich in his hand. On Charlie's question he returned it to the plate.

"Yeah," he said nervously, "she got away."

"No sense in asking for an autopsy then. You know how they are— Mrs. Crowley and Mrs. Langley. They love animals. They'd do anything to protect them."

"Yeah," the attendant managed.

"Where is he buried?"

"Buried?"

"Lorca."

The young man, opening a drawer, pulled from it a chain of dangling keys worthy of Old Bailey. He stood, eyed the Underwoods with suspicion. He started out. They followed.

The room he took them into was wide and empty. Cold, grey and friendless. The walls contained niches, mostly occupied with vases of one styling or another. He walked along the wall, slowly searching for the correct niche.

"Here we are," he said rather defiantly.

The niche was higher than head level, but the young man stood on his toes and took hold of the vessel and brought it to a small marble table near the door. With a finger he drew their attention to the inscription. Charlie read:

LORCA

Poet and dog

—Gina Langley

"Satisfied?" There was a hint of challenge in the way he spoke the word.

"Yes, thank you. You understand Mrs. Crowley—"

"Aw," interrupted the attendant, "no need to explain nothin' about her. I talked to her too many times. Couldn't prove if this puppy was poisoned now, could you?"

"The person that hit the dog—"

"I don't know nothin' about that person—look—I work for Mrs. Crowley, too. Y'know? I mean like I don't want to hurt my best customer. You tell her to call me if she wants anything else from Dreamy Pastures."

Charlie saw that further attempts to elicit information would get him nowhere. He thanked the attendant who showed them out, barely nodding in goodbye.

Driving back toward Mountain Shadows, Dolly asked some questions.

"How did you know that Dreamy Pastures was the right pet mortuary?"

"Lars. I telephoned him early this evening."

"Looks like a dead end."

"How do you mean?"

"You didn't find out anything."

"On the contrary, I found out everything I need to know at this point. A stroke of good fortune. Luck, if you will."

"I don't understand."

"I've been working on the assumption that both Lorca and Dorothea were taken to Dreamy Pastures. If Lorca hadn't been and we could find his burial spot then we could ask some potent questions."

"If the van didn't cart away Lorca—who was the passenger for the crematorium?"

"You're thinking clearly, dear."

"But what makes you think Lorca wasn't taken care of the same time Dorothea was?"

"Two reasons. The attendant's description of the hound. He accepted what I said. Short legs, big head. No, he never saw Lorca. You remember what strange canines they were. Tall, skin and bones, faces like foxes. Secondly, do you recall the name Lisa heard Mike use the first time she was aware of the phone call? He said a man's name. Is that you—?"

"Jerry! Is that you, Jerry?"

"I took one of the calling cards of House Gingerbread."

DREAMY PASTURES
Mr. and Mrs. E. Snowcroft, Mgrs.
Jerry Cox, Guest Relations

"I see," said Dolly, understanding. "Now what?"

"Find Lorca's grave. Face Mike with the evidence and see what he says. One other thing, too. About the hit-and-run driver. Jerry didn't say the driver got away. He said, 'she got away.' Interesting."

"I take it you have a plan?"

"I have."

A chilling desert breeze lapped over the car.

"*Brrrr*," Dolly said between her teeth. She snuggled close. Charlie kissed her forehead.

"We've got some place to go tonight."

She pulled away, disappointed.

"Don't worry, lamb," he said comfortingly, "I mean bed."

Chapter Eleven

"Really, Charles, can't you be less persistent?"

"I'm afraid I can't, Mrs. Langley—"

"Gina. I like those I like to call me Gina. Mrs. Langley has about it a quality of middle-age drabness. Don't you agree?"

"Haven't given the matter much thought."

They were in Gina's studio, a small place in contrast with other rooms in the house. She was working with mosaics, piecing the scraps of tile onto a large mural. The design was taking the shape of a large tiger. A Burmese cat was asleep on a stool next to the artist.

"Are you copying the cat?"

Gina laughed.

"No, Nhu-Nhu here likes to be close when I'm working. She's not in the least standoffish."

"About Miss Darnell—"

"I imagine she's off somewhere. We'll be hearing from her when she's ready to let us know where she is. Often does this type of thing. Dreadfully unreliable girl."

"I'm afraid I must insist. How did you happen to hire her?"

"Charles, she was an unimportant secretary, nothing more."

"That's how you thought of her?"

"Yes."

"Unimportant?"

"You're being rude."

Gina was dressed in a floral-print smock. Determinedly she thrust her hand in her pocket in search of a handkerchief. A nervous gesture and Charlie caught it.

"Unimportant? How is it, then, that she was on the Museum Board?"

Gina took a deep breath.

"Mr. Underwood, if you do not stop prying, I shall—"

"Call Inspector Van Spanckeren?"

Gina looked at him and in doing so betrayed her anxiety. She was deathly pale.

"I assure you Tod and I are doing everything we can to protect everyone concerned. You see, Gina, I don't believe Dorothea has gone anywhere. I have a hunch she was murdered. I also think Henry Ullman was murdered."

"Nonsense."

A scrap of tile fell to the floor, then another. Gina wasn't able to keep them in her hand.

"The phone calls about Snow White are not nonsense. The fact that Howard Stacey was poisoned—"

"An accident."

"Okay—Dorothea's disappearance means nothing. Ullman being slammed on the head with a bronze casting was an accident. Stacey being stung by a scorpion in a jar of dead scorpions was an oversight on his part. Carter Aubery getting a call telling him that Michael Jarvits loved Dorothea and believes Carter killed her is nonsense, too."

"All right, please—"

She sat on the stool next to Nhu-Nhu's.

"I've been trying to pretend that all this wasn't happening—"

"Gina, believe me when I say I want to help you."

"I—I believe you, but—"

"Tod and I will check any publicity. Remember, *you* may be next in line for an accident or an oversight."

She reached out and touched Charlie's hand for support, nodding that she understood.

"I didn't know who she was or anything about her. At first. We—we sometimes make mistakes, foolish ones. It's not the mistakes of significance that trap one, but the other—foolish ones. Like people. Only the fools and the ignorant can destroy you."

"I know this is hard for you."

Suddenly she brightened.

"Not at all, Charlie. What must be must be. A year ago, maybe less, I took a house in San Francisco. Sausalito—a little village over the Golden Gate, heading into Marin County. Lovely, on the water. And even Mother was—how shall I put it—less herself than usual, which was all to the good.

"There were many boats in the tiny harbor. I enjoyed walking along the pier. One was a yacht from Sweden. Handsome craft. I'm sorry if this sounds disorganized—I—I—I—"

"Tell it your own way."

"*The Astrid*. Yacht's name. One day I saw the owner. A handsome man, very Nordic, very exciting. Unfortunately for me, I was going through a Scandinavian phase in Sausalito. Reading Ibsen day and night, filling the house with flowers, eating heavy foods. And the skipper fitted in so nicely."

She had lowered her voice, allowing her hand to wander to Nhu-Nhu who was purring in response to her stroking.

"I was in La Jolla some months later when Miss Darnell appeared and applied for a position as my secretary. My *personal* secretary. She emphasized that word. I thought her fairly cheeky. She had an envelope with her and she left it on my desk. I was doing a monograph on the short plays of Cervantes at the time."

"What was in the envelope?"

"Photographs."

"I see. The skipper?"

"I was to find out in time that he took charge of the yacht during the winter. The yacht's owner was in Canada. Larry—that was his name—Larry was what one might call a glorified cabin boy."

She spoke the last bitterly.

"So it was either hire Dorothea or—"

"She'd peddle the—photographs. Not really peddle them. As I remember, she said the photographs would merely reveal me for what I was."

"A charmer, wasn't she."

"I couldn't risk what she threatened. I am part of this town. My late husband had dignity here. I have dignity here. If I were younger, much younger, I would have told her to do with those photographs as she chose and damn any repercussions. But I am too old. Too old even for Larry. I had my charities here, the new museum. My work and contributions for the community. However, I had no intention of letting her get away with it. That's why I took her on. To keep my eye on her. To decide what would have to be done.

"I planned to give her – what is that expression? – ah, yes – enough rope to hang herself."

Charlie listened with no display of emotion.

"I'm told people murder for one of three reasons, is that correct, Charles?"

"I would have to hear the reasons."

"Jealousy."

"A good motive."

"Profit."

"Also true."

"Revenge."

"They're real good."

"I certainly wasn't jealous of her. I suppose profit might enter into it. I would lose nothing by her death, and gain a kind of safety. But revenge would be my motive, wouldn't it? That is, if I had murdered her. I assumed, when she disappeared, that she had returned to her cabin boy. *That swine.* Forgive me if I sound unladylike."

Whatever Gina Langley said, it sounded ladylike.

"I could have handled her myself. After she came here to Phoenix and got somewhat established she broke down and cried. Gave me some story of a hard life, said she did what she did because she was desperate. I half believed her. Especially when she produced the negatives and let me burn them.

"But in a week or so the reason for this was plain. She was blackmailing everyone she could. My friends. That angered me. Greatly. So, Charles, I stand before you naked, as it were. I could have murdered her—"

"Did you, Gina? Did you murder Dorothea Darnell?"

"No, Charles, I did not."

"Do you know who did?"

"That's presumptuous, but to answer your question – *if* little Snow White has been murdered, I do not know who the murderer is."

"Could be anyone, then. Anyone who ever came in contact with her?"

"I should think so."

Nhu-Nhu stretched, stiffening her hind legs as she did so.

"That night – the night before Dorothea dropped from sight – your dog – "

"Lorca?"

"The Ibizan, yes. How did he die?"

The expression on Gina's face froze.

"My mother is an elderly woman. When people become her age, they develop childish habits. Petulance, among them. There was an argument. I went to bed. An hour later she was still fuming, backed out the car, started down the road. Lorca ran after the car, got in front of it and—"

"How did you find out about it?"

"Next morning at breakfast, she told me. Poor thing was contrite, sad. She can break a heart at times. She had called the animal man from the pet mortuary – I have an account – and he took poor Lorca away before I knew anything about his demise. Better that way, I think. Poor Mama—she was so depressed."

They talked a little after this and Charles left Mrs. Langley with the understanding she was to call if anything turned up.

On his way out, he encountered the peacock and Mrs. Crowley.

"Howdy-doo," she said in greeting.

"Fine and you?"

"Been better."

She was dressed conservatively in a dress befitting her advanced age.

"I see the Oriental phase has passed."

"What?"

The peacock was on a string and resented it. He made a frightful racket.

"Things aren't coming up Chinatown anymore."

"Do I want to go to Chinatown? There's no Chinatown in Phoenix. I don't eat chop suey. I like Mexican food. Gina's having the whole house done in Spanish Colonial."

Charlie sighed. The old woman had gotten her time sequences mixed and didn't recall that the Spanish Colonial phase had come and gone.

"How's that girl who dances?"

"Fine, thanks."

"When's the wedding?"

"Wedding?"

"When are you going to marry her?"

Charlie gave up.

He said goodbye to the old woman and headed out for his car.

"I'll see you at your office. At the museum," she yelled as he went on. He turned once. The peacock had gotten free and the old lady was chasing him.

At his car, Charlie laughed. "Good grief," he thought to himself. "She thinks I'm Michael Jarvits."

Then an idea occurred.

The body of the dead man lay beneath a white sheet. In the icy room, footsteps echoed. A morgue attendant stood at the head of the dead man, waiting to pull back the sheet. The setting was reminiscent of the Dreamy Pastures mortuary. Even that same dreadful smell of disinfectant lingered.

"I thought you would want to know," said Van Spanckeren. "In a sense, you were working for him, weren't you?"

"In a sense."

Tod stood on one side of the table, Charlie on the other. The attendant awaited instructions.

"Guy – like this," Tod said sadly. "Everything in the world – why would he commit suicide?"

He lifted a finger and the white-jacketed attendant lifted the sheet.

Carter Aubery looked very much as a corpse should.

"When did it happen?"

"Some time last evening. About midnight."

Van Spanckeren indicated that the attendant should leave the friendless room and the man did so.

"Had you talked to him since the night you were there – at his place?"

"No."

"Know anyone who might have?"

"No. Turning into quite a case, isn't it? The museum crowd. Stacey stung by a scorpion. An *accident*, I guess."

"He's fine now. Poison out, body fit."

"I'm glad to hear it. Ullman's *accident*— "

"I'm inclined to think there might be some merit in your theory about Hank Ullman."

"What makes you think that?"

He looked down at the corpse.

"This suicide."

He lifted a corner of the sheet and exposed the wrist of the dead man.

"Carter slashed his wrists. Thin razor blade. Here, look."

Charlie looked, saying, "Very neat, very deliberate."

"Do you see anything unusual about that?"

"At the moment, no."

"You haven't seen many suicides then?"

"To be honest – none."

"I have, unfortunately. When they choose to do it this way, they're always hesitant and there's one characteristic that stands out – hesitation marks. The suicide never makes one clear cut. He or she starts out with tiny slashes, testing, building courage, then the fatal slash. But here, there is just one steady line across the veins in each wrist. Too neat. I'll stake my credentials that someone did this for Carter. Murder."

"Any clues?"

"None whatsoever. There's no doorman at the Towers. Elevator is self-operating. Carter knew who his – murderer – was. No sign of a struggle. Nothing taken. Lab analysis showed he was well-oiled – excuse me – he'd had plenty to drink."

"He may have passed out."

"I think he did. He liked to put it away."

"Next step?"

Tod Van Spanckeren dropped the sheet back into position, a mite squeamishly, Charlie thought.

"I was hoping we could pool resources. Together we might hit on something."

"We might."

"If Ullman's death was murder, Stacey's misfortune attempted murder, this suicide a fake—"

"Someone else may be in line?"

"Never dismiss a possibility. What do you say?"

"I'm intrigued by your change in attitude. Amazing what a few hesitation marks will accomplish."

Tod Van Spanckeren was worried. This showed on his face.

"It isn't this death alone."

"What – specifically?"

"I had a conversation with Mrs. Langley yesterday. Her telephone's been buzzing again."

"Snow White?"

"Not this time. She couldn't be certain it was the same voice. This time he didn't ask any question, but laid it on the line."

Charles said nothing, allowing Van Spanckeren to tell it his own way. The police inspector kept looking at Charlie and then down to the sheeted corpse.

"He said Mike Jarvits was out for revenge. That Mike thought the museum crowd was somehow mixed in with Dorothea Darnell's—"

He stopped, as if he hoped Charlie would supply the missing word. Charlie remained silent.

" –death. He said 'death.' Caller also said he was telling this to Gina because Mike would probably try to get at her. The pieces are jagged and jagged pieces can cut. That worries me."

His expression brightened.

"What do you say?"

"About your theory?"

"About us working together."

In his own mind, Charlie had a reservation or two regarding the affable inspector. Yet, he couldn't refuse entirely. He decided he would let the policeman in on much of what he suspected. Not all.

"Come on," Charlie said in a friendly manner. "I'll buy you a cup of coffee."

The Leopard Woman was sitting on the edge of the pool, her long limbs dipping in the water. Two salesmen from Butte, Montana, were in the pool and they kept a running conversation going. The Leopard Woman would giggle from time to time.

Dolly sat in the shade of the patio's ramada, filing her nails and eavesdropping. She was wearing her pink swimsuit and the Filipino waiters were polishing the rail of the terrace walls and poking each other.

There was a squeal from the pool. The salesman had managed to grab the Leopard Woman by the leg and pull her in. When her hair bobbed above the water, its long blackness caught the shimmering of the sun.

The telephone rang and Dolly entered the cabana.

"Hello."

"This the lady that was out to Dreamy Pastures Pet Mortuary?"

"I was out there with my husband. Yesterday."

"Underwood?"

"Yes."

"I gotta speak to him."

"He's not here at the moment. Could I take—?"

The man rang off. He had sounded scared, but Dolly had clearly recognized the voice of Jerry Cox.

Chapter Twelve

"Mirror, mirror on the wall; who is fairest of them all?"

"*You* are, Dolly Underwood."

Charlie was flat on his back in bed; Dolly was seated before a vanity. She had been brushing her hair and it fell softly to her shoulders. Charlie preferred it longish. Short hairstyles he found unappealing, and Dolly was one woman who dressed to please her husband. Even the negligee confirmed this, being theatrical to a fault. Sheer, deep navy, trimmed with ribbons and strings.

Charlie was bare-chested. He ran his hand over his flat stomach as he studied the card.

"First card takes care of itself. Snow White was a vicious blackmailer who used Gina to get into a very profitable crowd. As far as the drug is concerned, it's DLS, lysergic acid diethylamide. Two people on the board have not been touched: Mrs. Crowley and daughter. As for the informant who was spreading gossip about Mike Jarvits, he may or may not be the same character who's been dishing out with the Grimm's."

"You still haven't been able to reach Jerry Cox?" said Dolly, in front of the mirror.

"It was *Cox*? No doubt in your mind?"

"Darling, it sounded like him. I think as you do, since I've become your loving wife."

"How's that?"

"Either it was Mr. Cox or a person who sounded like him."

"A most perceptive attempt to discover my methods," he said jovially. "When I called Dreamy Pastures the old woman who answered said she hadn't seen him since early morning. He may have blown town."

"What a vulgar expression."

"He may have left town."

"That's much better. Charlie—"

"Hmmmm?"

"You don't think Jerry Cox has been – killed?"

"I don't know."

Dolly left the vanity and came to the bed, taking on Charlie's chore of massaging his belly.

"I thought what Lisa said about Mike resigning was sad. She thought she was at the end of the rainbow. Mike'll have to start all over again. At the bottom."

He sat up, bracing his back against two pillows. Dolly ceased massaging.

"Dolly, how well do you know your old dancing friend?"

"Huh?"

"Lisa"

"What do you mean—"

"Just answer the question."

"I knew her quite well in New York, Charlie. I told you about her – what a scatterbrain she was then. 'Course that was some years ago. She's matured."

"What was she after – in New York?"

"I don't think she knew. I'm not certain any of us did."

She winked at her husband.

"Every woman wants the same thing, beast."

He took her in his arms, letting his right hand wander over her body.

"What things?" he said in a low, throaty whisper.

"We all want a Charlie Underwood."

"Then you don't think she's a terribly jealous woman?"

Disgruntled, Dolly pulled away.

"Charlie, you have the world's worse sense of timing."

"What are you talking about?"

"I'm talking about you. Every time things start to get romantic and lovely, that mathematical brain starts punching holes in an IBM card."

She walked back to the vanity and once again began to brush her hair. This time with short, swift movements.

"If you mean," she said heatedly, "do I think she's mixed in with this museum thing, no. Besides, if she were jealous of Dorothea, the person to kill would not be Carter, Ullman or Stacey, or anyone like that. If she were that jealous, she'd murder Doro—"

She broke off on the second syllable, her brushing stopped, and she paled.

"Oh, God, Charlie, you don't think that."

Flatly, he replied: "I didn't say a thing, beauty, *you* did."

"I can't believe anything like that about—"

"That's the great ally of evil, wife, the fact that most people can't believe in it."

"Not *her*."

"Stop worrying. She's no more open to suspicion than anyone else."

"Ah, but I know you. You're a great exponent of Napoleonic law—"

"What are you babbling about?"

"Guilty until proven innocent." She started brushing again, her strokes regulated.

She said: "You mean you have some plan, don't you?"

"I have one, a gamble all the way."

Dolly turned.

"What is it?"

"There's one question that is still wide open—"

"Which is?"

"Where is Snow White buried?"

"I thought we confirmed that. Dreamy Pastures."

"Perhaps, but tonight I think we'll get to the point. There's a size-able drawback, though. A rough one."

"How rough?"

"Gina Langley."

"I hate to sound insistent, darling, but would you please tell me what's going on?"

"I called Gina this afternoon. Talked to her for some time. I think she trusts me. I hope so, for her sake as well as my own. We're wait-ing for a telephone call, Dolly. It'll come soon if everything goes the way I plan. Get dressed."

"I don't understand—"

"I'll explain it on our way to Gina's."

"Back to the fun house?"

Charlie swung his legs to the floor and reached for his shoes un-der the bed. Dolly went to the closet and selected a knit suit, turning sharply on Charlie's cry.

"My God, what is it?" Her face was ashen.

Charlie held his shoe in his right hand and motioned Dolly to his side. The creature was tiny, cruel, infuriated, racing around the arena of the shoe in a frantic effort to escape, the tall pitching back and forth, as if to strike.

To Dolly, the thing looked like a lobster, a microscopic, agitated lobster.

"Scorpion," Charlie said.

"Are you sure?"

"Yes." He turned over the shoe and the creature dropped to the carpet, crushed a second later by a fast blow with the other shoe. There was a sickly odor.

Charlie took an envelope from the desk and brushed the dead thing inside. Dolly looked away.

"About how long were we outside at the pool this afternoon?"

"A couple of hours."

"Long enough for anyone to come in here without our seeing them."

Half an hour later the expected call came.

The main gate was open and they rode along the dusty route to Gina Langley's casa silently, but instead of driving onto the driveway in front of the building, Charlie stopped the car some distance away.

"On foot from here on in, baby."

Dolly stepped from the car and looked about. It wouldn't have surprised her at all if a phantom sprang. Charlie had opened the trunk of the car.

"What are you doing?"

"I made a purchase at a nursery this morning. Time to put it to work."

He had a new shovel in his hand.

"What's that for?"

He slammed down the trunk.

"Curiosity killed the cat."

"Yes," answered Dolly with a touch of sarcasm, "but information brought her back."

They walked cautiously toward the house. There were many lights on, though they did not appear inviting.

Charlie took his wife's hand, walking in silence.

Easily they found their way to the inner patio of birds. The cages were there, but the macaws and parrots were not.

"Like in Lars' painting," whispered Dolly. "This was his setting. I didn't realize it. Right down to the empty cages."

"Be quiet."

He checked his watch.

"What are we waiting for?"

"Quiet."

In less than five minutes, Gina Langley in a silk slack outfit, look-ing like a thin Jean Harlow, came into the patio. They were hidden in the shadows. There was no moon and, because of the arrangement of the house, no illumination spilled into the patio.

Charlie said, "We're here, Mrs. Langley."

Breathily, Gina replied, "Where? I can't see you."

Charlie stepped from the shadows.

"Oh, I feared I had gotten your instructions wrong."

"He's here?"

"Yes, he's been here for some time."

"And your mother?"

Gina's throat went dry, words were difficult to project.

"She's—"

"She did go somewhere? Somewhere on the grounds?"

"I can't believe—"

"Remember what I said, Gina, you've got to trust in me—"

"She's gone onto the desert, to the east. A small bird sanctuary there. A statue of Saint Anthony feeding birds—"

"How can I get there?"

"Go out front, turn right, follow the side of the house until you come to the garage, behind the garage, again to the right, look east—you can't miss the spot. The statue is lighted."

"Good. Remember, I want—"

"Ten minutes."

"Check. It's eleven twenty now. I want you and your guest at that bird sanctuary on the dot at eleven thirty."

Gina nodded reluctantly, turned, started out, paused, turned back, made to say something and promptly changed her mind. She left the patio.

"Frightened?"

"To be honest – yes!"

"Sssh."

"What are we going to find?"

"If I knew, darling, we wouldn't be going through this charade."

He took her hand again. She felt safer.

Charlie followed Gina's instructions. Leaving the patio, they continued on out to the front and then turned right, walking cautiously along the side of the house. They came to the garage, turning right once again and they were behind it. In the near distance, they could see the lighted statue and beside it the figure of a woman.

Dolly squeezed her husband's hand.

"Charlie, this is weird. Let's get out of here."

She squeezed tighter.

"Charlie, who is she? Do you know?"

"Yes, and so do you."

As they neared the sanctuary, identifying the woman was easy.

She stood nervously, peering at the visitors through the darkness. But she couldn't make them out. The lighted area put her in a position that made seeing beyond the ring of illumination difficult. She, however, was easy to make out from the darker vantage points.

Some distance from her, Charlie stopped.

"That you?"

Charlie did not respond.

"Crazy," said the figure, "crazy. Why do you want to go over this again? Forget it. Like we said. We all promised. Forget it. What's the matter? Why don't you say something?"

Mrs. Crowley's voice was tinged with apprehension and confusion.

"Who's there?" she asked again, frightened.

"The man who called you, Mrs. Crowley."

"I know, but what do you want? Why here?"

Dolly had goose bumps.

Mrs. Crowley panicked.

"I'm going to get my daughter."

"No need to do that, Mrs. Crowley. She'll be here shortly."

Charlie and Dolly stepped forward. Mrs. Crowley looked surprised. She furrowed her brow.

"Are you the one from the museum?"

"Yes, don't you recall? We talked not too long ago. You asked me when I was going to marry the dancer."

Demented as she was, Mrs. Crowley could smell a rat.

Forcefully, she declared, "You're not him."

She started to hurry away, but Charlie took her gently by the arm. He felt as if he were holding the twig of a tree.

"There's nothing to worry about. Your daughter and Mr. Jarvits will be here in a moment."

A few minutes following, they were.

Both Gina and Mike were distressed. When Mike saw the trio he started to turn.

"*Mike*," commanded Charlie.

Jarvits turned back, his eyes haunted.

"What the hell is all this about?"

"Where is Snow White buried?"

Mrs. Crowley stepped toward her daughter. Gina appeared to understand little of what was transpiring.

"What the hell are you talking about?"

"I think you know. Dreamy Pastures, Jerry Cox, Lorca—"

Gina repeated the dog's name. "Lorca?"

Charlie continued to look at Jarvits.

"I've been to Dreamy Pastures, Mike. I've talked to Jerry Cox—"

Mike was sweating. Visibly.

"He's disappeared, Mike. Jerry's disappeared. The night Lorca was hit by a car you rode with the driver to Dreamy Pastures, didn't you?"

There was a cold look in Mike's eyes.

"Strange thing to do, escort a dog to a pet cemetery. It was a dog, wasn't it?"

"Yes," Jarvits mouthed as if in pain.

"Lorca?"

"Y-yes, Lorca."

"No, it wasn't Lorca. Jerry Cox never saw Lorca. And if he didn't – who was in that van? Dorothea Darnell!"

"No!"

"And if Dorothea was cremated in place of Lorca and Lorca was not taken to Dreamy Pastures, where is he buried? Because if he is buried *here*, something, someone took his place in the van."

Mike began to protest, erratic, disconnected. "That's foolish—ridiculous—who saw me in that van—nonsense—it was Lorca."

Charlie picked up the shovel and dug the tip of it into the soil. The ground was not hard. Mrs. Crowley began to whimper, pitiably.

"All I have to do," stated Charlie, "is dig."

An agonized "No" sprang from Jarvits' throat. Only a stony heart could fail to feel some pity for the man.

"Don't! He's buried where you're standing. Right where you're standing."

"Lorca?"

"Yes, the dog. Lorca."

Mrs. Crowley dissolved into tears; Gina Langley promptly fainted.

They were in the gallery room. Gina was stretched out on her favorite sofa, looking languidly out the large window and into the inner patio.

The Ibizan hounds were curious about the activity within. They stood outside the glass panes, noses pressed against the window, tails wagging, eyes alert.

Juan, the butler, had brought in coffee. Gina had drunk several cups. She was feeling better. Michael Jarvits stood by the room's large hearth. Mrs. Crowley was seated in a high-winged-back chair. Charlie stood by the sofa, Dolly sat on an ottoman.

"I want to repeat again," said Charlie, "that I *had* to take a course like this. No one was being honest. Everyone was worried, yet no one would admit to anything, although the innuendoes weren't scarce. Want to tell me about it?"

Mike tapped out a cigarette from a pack, lit it, took a deep puff and said, "What difference does it make now?"

He walked toward Gina.

"About Dorothea - I don't know much about her, you've discovered - that is—"

"I've learned quite a bit about the lady in question, from varied sources."

Michael Jarvits looked at his employer uneasily, but Gina gave no sign of understanding Charlie's remark. The detective saw the byplay and wasn't impressed. He was in no mood to coddle sensitivities.

"I wasn't referring to Mrs. Langley alone."

Gina took a deep breath.

"There's Carter—"

Gina held up her hand in protest. "Please, let's not discuss poor Aubery. We've had a service for Henry, barely a few days ago, and now—I shall have to officiate all over again."

"I think that's a very slight problem. At the moment I'm not interested in Carter Aubery, except to say he, too, was being blackmailed by Miss Darnell."

Gina said nonchalantly, "I didn't know."

"Lars Waddington, the same. And if I checked around I'm confident Howard Stacey or anyone else connected with the museum would be able to tell the same story."

Mike made a fist with his right hand and slammed it into the palm of his left.

"Damn," he exclaimed, cuttingly, "I had no idea she was so good at organization – but then -- why not?"

"Everyone's being most gentlemanly and ladylike and I am most impressed. If you don't care to tell me, Mike, there's always the police."

Mike Jarvits sat on the ottoman next to Dolly's.

"Yes," he said, the word muffled. "Blackmail."

"Didn't have anything on me, the bitch," rasped Mrs. Crowley in triumph.

"*Mother!*"

"She didn't!"

"All right!" cut in Gina, "she didn't. Go on, Mike."

"The thing about Dorothea was her manner. You never could tell whether she was being victimized or whether you were. She had a knack of finding out what a person's weak spots were. She was indiscreet, charming, lovable – in a detached manner. I never knew what she was about until it was too late, and even then I couldn't believe it. She wore such a fine coat of respectability. She was mechanically inclined. Did you know?"

"Mind repeating that?"

"She knew how to work tiny Japanese tape recorders. The kind you could slip behind a pillow or put in a flower vase."

"Sweet child."

"She played everyone for what she could get. That was her magic quality. When she came to me with the tapes she kept saying she hoped I understood; that she had to do it. Her life was a variation on the Little Match Girl – according to her. Said it would break her heart to give the tapes to Lisa."

"The *minx*," exclaimed a most indignant Dolly.

"Understand – the tapes, after a few drinks, well – I wouldn't want anyone to hear them. There were other things, too. Remarks I made about Carter Aubery, the running of the museum and—"

He broke off and looked at Gina Langley.

"—there were also some exceptions I made to Mrs. Langley's ability and personality. My personal life would be a shambles if anyone, Lisa especially, heard them. As for my career – after my frank evaluation of my employers – that, too, would be finished. There was a letter I had written to her. Might say I was in a terribly romantic mood. A lesson a man should learn by heart – never put anything in writing."

"Where is the letter?"

"She said someone had stolen it. Holding it in reserve, I imagine, for future requests."

"How much did she want?"

Mike laughed out of the corner of his mouth, sardonically.

"She knew what my salary was. Said she wanted to be fair. All she

wanted was one thousand dollars in cash and an occasional painting before it was catalogued. Occasional paintings that wouldn't
attract much attention by their absence. You see, Snow White had
an eye to the future."

Gina stood and began to pace.

"This is my fault. *Mine*. I have principles and I'm strong. I should
have turned her over to the police the instant she came to me with
her threats. No, oh, no. I couldn't do that. My reputation, my ego.
I am guilty."

She returned to the sofa and sat with a sigh.

"I accept my guilt," she announced.

Mike said, "Gina, this is no time for existentialistic philosophy."

"She didn't have anything on me. I'm clean."

"Yes, Mother."

"That night—" Charlie began, "the night of Lorca's death, what
happened?"

Gina began, cutting off Mike.

"I have been tremendously interested in drugs that free the creative
spirit. Nothing common, you understand. I do admit I have tried a
variety of hallucinogenic drugs in the hopes of achieving a mystical
experience. On weekends a friend connected with a research foun-
dation often came here. Some of my more creative friends entered
into the experiments."

"DLS?"

"Yes, Mr. Underwood."

"Addicts!" bellowed Mrs. Crowley.

Gina was losing her patience.

"In pill form. Effects last about eight hours. My friend was always
here to supervise and keep a journal. Thrilling. I was able to watch flowers breathe, sounds speak. And when the initial effect ended, I was able
to paint, write, compose. My head had been cleansed of obstacles.

"Mind you, the people selected were of a special, dear me – I don't
want to use the word 'class'— "

"Artistic nature," supplied Mike.

"Excellent. All of an artistic nature. Dorothea was fascinated by the experiments. She told me once she wished to experience every thrill and emotion life had to offer. She was desperate to take part in the experiments, but my friend from the Research Institute was not interested in her. This naturally infuriated her.

"One evening – I believe it was Carter – yes, Carter took the experiment. Later that night my friend got a plane back to the Institute, but he left a bottle of pills, or so I thought. As I say, they should only be taken with supervision.

"She confronted me after my guests had gone, Dorothea. Said my friend had not left the pills at all, that she had taken them from his overnight bag. She then vilified me; said people like me always hated people like her. That's interesting, I think, since at the moment her observation was painfully true.

"To show she could have anything she wanted, when she chose, she uncapped the bottle and swallowed several of the pills. The whole bottle, perhaps."

"Dangerous?"

"Extremely. There's considerable debate on its merit. DLS. People who are schizophrenic or unbalanced may suffer – delusions of one sort or another. A new drug, not fully tested—"

"Didn't you call a doctor?"

"No."

"Shouldn't you have?"

Quietly, the woman replied, "I suppose at various times in my life I should have or should not have done many things. With Dorothea I subconsciously – to be polite about it – hoped the drugs would help her to experience every emotion, including that final one."

Charlie turned toward Mrs. Crowley. She looked at him squarely and didn't wait for him to ask any question. Her speech was rational and coherent.

"I was angry with Gina. I'm afraid of drugs, things like that. But

I can tell a vulture when one nests. First time I saw that Dorothea, I said to myself, 'Take care, lady, take care.' She didn't fool me with her saucer eyes and Bo Peep ways.

"I took a walk along the road. Often do that when I want to get tired. Helps me to sleep. Lorca was walking with me. I heard this roar. A car came screeching down the driveway and into the road. Dorothea must have been riding eighty miles an hour. Fast. Never saw no one drive like that. I thought I was going to the big dance palace in the sky, I did. Instead of me, it was poor puppy dog. She slammed square into a date tree and finished herself off but good.

"I'm a good mother. If there was publicity Gina would suffer. My girl don't like publicity, not *that* kind. I got hold of Mike and he came out, and my friend at the pet cemetery—"

"Jerry Cox?"

"That's the boy. Wild boy. I knew money would appeal to him. He wants to buy that business. Told me so. Told me if I ever knew of any good deals to tip him off. I tipped him off, I did."

"Why did you call Mike?"

"I couldn't call anyone else. He lived alone. He worked for Gina—"

Mike said, "I kept telling myself I wanted the position at the museum. I'd be the youngest museum director in the country. That appealed, Charlie. Too, I suppose, in a way, I was glad to see the end of *Snow White*."

He said her nickname scornfully.

"I'm always banging the car to bits," Mrs. Crowley said rather proudly. "So no one thought anything about it when they saw it next morning."

All at once her energy and alertness faded. She brought her hand to her forehead.

"I'm tired. I want to go to bed."

She started out.

"I'm going to have Juan fix me an avocado sandwich with bacon.

That's what I'll do."

She slowly made her way from the room. No one spoke. A wind whirled in the inner patio making dust devils in the dark.

"She – has a good heart," said Gina.

"There you have it," said Mike. "This wrap it up for you?"

Gina looked helpless.

"I want to make a request. I would like both of you to mention nothing of this to anyone until I give the word." Before they could say anything Charlie continued on. "Mike, did you and Mrs. Crowley exchange words after that night?"

"Not a single word. I was afraid Mrs. Crowley might slip. But I never heard a word about the matter. I was hoping it was forgotten."

"Jerry would know."

"Yes, he would."

"I'd like to continue on this case. We know about Dorothea. Yet—"

He thought of mentioning Ullman, Stacey, and Aubery, all victims, even the scorpion in his shoe, but thought better of it.

"What will happen to us?"

"Gina, you're not guilty of anything."

She seemed disappointed.

"Perhaps you are now," added Charlie as an afterthought. "We all are. Concealing a death. I believe I can help you both. Will you follow my instructions explicitly these next few days?"

Gina and Michael nodded agreement.

Shortly thereafter, the Underwoods returned to Mountain Shadows.

The answers, despite the evening's success, continued to elude.

Chapter Thirteen

Mr. Jenckes, Henry Ullman's law partner, listened attentively.

Charlie sat in front of the attorney's desk trying to make his request sound natural, though he knew perfectly well this wasn't the case.

"If I understand you correctly, Mr. Underwood, and I think I do, you want me to betray my professional ethics."

"Mr. Jenckes, those two words have always troubled me. Betray and ethics."

"If what you suggest is possible, why isn't this entire affair a matter for the police?"

"I think you know the answer to that."

"What about Inspector Van Spanckeren?"

"We're working on this together. You're free to call him if you mistrust me."

"Not a question of trusting or mistrusting. If you want to know what's in Mrs. Langley's will, why don't you ask her to tell you?"

"You've dealt with the woman far longer than I have—"

"This law office has. Mrs. Langley came to be my default, one might say. Because of Henry's unfortunate accident."

"If you insist – accident."

"Officially it is, despite your suspicion. As for poor Carter—"

"I should hate to hear you say, 'Poor Mrs. Langley'."

"You really believe she may be in danger?"

"I do."

"And you won't let me call to get her permission?"

"I prefer that you didn't. As I started to say a moment ago, Mrs. Langley can be – how shall I say – 'devious' doesn't express what I want."

"Difficult?"

"Perfect. Difficult. If I asked to see her will, she's very likely to say she lost it. If I asked her to tell me what was in it, she might lie. Playfully, of course, but it would throw me off the track."

"What you say is true."

"Tell me this – has she changed her will? Recently?"

"Eight years ago she made a will. The original has not been altered with the exception of a few times."

Charlie was interested in this last remark.

"Then it *has* been changed."

"The basic will has not, but Gina has acquired new properties over those eight years. The changes in the will concern these. Not changes at all. Codicils."

"Mr. Jenckes, let me put it to you directly. I firmly believe that what you decide about letting me see the document has direct bearing on whether Gina Langley lives or dies."

A wild stab, but it looked as if it might work. Mr. Jenckes spun around in his swivel chair and pretended to stare out the window. He spun back and flipped a switch on his intercom.

"Miss Talbot, are you at your desk?"

"Yes, Mr. Jenckes," came a cheery lilt of a voice.

"Good, stay there."

Mr. Jenckes heaved himself from his chair and walked out of the office. This maneuver worried Charlie. What was he going to do? Call Gina? Van Spanckeren?

Suddenly the lawyer's office reminded him of a doctor's waiting room. He was crammed in, the room was stuffy. Where was Jenckes?

The door opened and a young woman, Miss Talbot, Charlie guessed, poked in her head and smiled.

"Mr. Jenckes says he'll be right along. Please wait."

Charlie said he would, she smiled again and left the room.

A good fifteen minutes had elapsed between the time Jenckes left the office and his return. He looked somber and troubled. There was a bulky file under his arm. He walked behind his desk, but did not sit down.

"Please do not misunderstand, Mr. Underwood. I consider much of what transpires between a client and his lawyer like what passes in a confessional. However, I am not insensitive or fanatical. If Mrs. Langley's life were in danger and I could—"

"I'm grateful."

"I'm afraid you persist in misunderstanding. I am not going to tell you what's in her will."

Charlie's heart began to sink.

"Nor am I going to hand you a copy."

"Sorry you feel this way. I do have Gina's interest at heart."

"Still – if I were to have a copy of the will on my desk, in this file for example, and I were to leave this office to confer with my secretary, I technically have violated no trust."

Mr. Jenckes may not have been a Philadelphia lawyer, but he assuredly was a Phoenix rationalist.

"Technically," Charles said, "you'd be correct."

Mr. Jenckes leaned over his desk and flipped on his intercom for a second time during Charlie's visit.

"Miss Talbot, are you at your desk?"

Again the bird song: "Yes, Mr. Jenckes."

He snapped a button to break the connection.

"I have some business to attend to, Mr. Underwood. I'll be outside for the next five minutes. I do make myself clear?"

"Thank you."

Mr. Jenckes said nothing further. He left.

Charlie snatched the file. The will was on top. Quickly he cut through the legalistic rigmarole and came to the additions Jenckes had mentioned. Whatever was to be found would be with the added clauses. He came to the odd provision regarding her paintings and Carter Aubery, and then he saw what he was looking for. He read this part carefully, twice.

Mr. Jenckes returned. "I'm sorry I couldn't be of any help to you, Mr. Underwood," he said, one hand holding the door ajar.

Charlie closed the file and put it back atop the desk.

"So am I," he answered.

Charlie paused at the door.

"One question – I've been wondering. Apart from anyone in this law office – would anyone have had an opportunity to see what I might have seen?"

"Secrecy and discretion are highly valued here, Mr. Underwood. To answer your question – *no one.*"

Charlie started to ask something else, but changed his mind.

"Goodbye," said Mr. Jenckes.

"Goodbye."

They did not shake hands.

The Underwoods spent the afternoon at the pool side.

"Know something, Charlie?"

"I know a lot of things."

"I mean about this valley. I think it's an island."

He was flat on his stomach, feeling the sun warm his back. Dolly was seated in a bamboo chair, her legs stretched to touch his head.

"An island?"

"I don't mean it's a physical island, but that it has island attributes. Like island fever. When a person doesn't want to do anything but sit around and laze in the sun."

"Sounds lovely to me."

"I think that's what I've got, Charlie. Island fever."

He was half-dozing.

"Charlie--?"

"Yes, baby?"

"Do you think we're getting anywhere with this museum business? I don't like to mention it, but you don't have a client. A paying one."

He yawned. "The memorial service is tomorrow at ten – guess where?"

"The museum."

"Right."

"The same routine? Probably the same ashes to be carried up to the Shelly Room."

Lazily, he mouthed, "No, the body was shipped to Illinois. Relatives. The service is going to be simple—"

"But effective. It *will* be that if Gina's in on it. Are you going?"

"Naturally. Don't you want to come along?"

"Would you be terribly offended if I didn't?"

"No, but I thought you'd want to be there."

"Once was enough."

Charlie looked upward to the terrace and squinted.

"Hey, where's your cheering section?"

Dolly frowned.

"When the Leopard Woman's around, no female stands a chance."

Charlie raised himself on an elbow and looked in the direction his wife pointed: the tennis court. The Leopard Woman in abbreviated shorts and tight-fitting white blouse was playing a match with a muscular male guest. She was something of an expert. The waiters were assembled on the edge of the terrace closest to the court.

"I see what you mean."

He was fascinated by the players' athletic prowess.

"Something of a classical Amazon, isn't she?"

Dolly tilted her foot under his chin.

"Don't squint in the sunlight, dear," she admonished, "you'll damage the retina."

He laughed and rolled onto his back.

"Charlie, I thought you were terribly clever last evening at Gina's. I'm sure they're all terrified of you. You're something of a magician."

"Why do you say that?"

"The way you figured it all out."

"You could have done the same, sweetheart. Rather simple."

"I dislike playing Watson to your Holmes."

"Lars definitely saw Mike in the van. He tried to pretend the man might have been someone else, but his intent was pointed. Had to be either Dorothea or Lorca in the van or both, but since Jerry Cox plainly never saw the dog, it was equally plain Lorca was buried elsewhere and someone had taken his place in the urn. Find Lorca and prove the ashes at Dreamy Pastures weren't his. Gina said her mother said Lorca had been taken away—therefore Mrs. Crowley was in on it. Mike in the van. Two and two. Confront at the grave of Lorca and they'd break, which they did. All I did was call the old woman, tell her I was Mike, the man at the museum, and to meet me at the grave at such and such a time. Told Gina to invite Mike to the house. Gina watched her mother, told me, brought Mike along in a few minutes. I gambled that the grave would be on the grounds."

"I admire you, Blackstone. But as you said last night—there are many things unsolved."

"Unsolved *and* unsaid. Those are the most dangerous, pet. Things unsaid."

"What do you make of Mrs. Crowley?"

"That's a silly question if ever there was one."

Dolly looked at her husband with disapproval.

"I don't mean her oddities. What interests me is the way she's perfectly lucid and alert one minute, then—to be blunt—very senile the next."

"For a dame her age, I think Mrs. Crowley is a remarkable dish."

"I'll go along with that. Senility, as far as I'm concerned, is an individual matter. It may be a defense, Charles."

"How so?"

"Anytime she wants to forget something or pretend she doesn't understand something, she falls back on her age."

"Possibly."

"Took a sharp mind to think as fast as she did about disposing of Snow White's body, calling Mike and paying off Jerry Cox."

"Food for thought."

Charlie was not paying her much mind and she was annoyed.

"What's on the docket for today?" she said quickly.

"Nothing. Tomorrow, after the service, I'm taking some people to lunch."

"Who?"

"Mrs. Crowley."

"Oh, delightful."

"Lars Waddington and Howard Stacey."

"I take it there's a method in your madness."

"By the time we're on coffee, I hope there'll be."

"And *tonight* – what are we going to do to amuse ourselves to-night?"

Charlie rolled back on his belly and in doing so he seized his wife's ankle. She was delighted.

"Tonight I'm taking you for cocktails on the desert, then dinner, than dancing. How's that sound?"

"Charlie," she hissed suggestively, "will you marry me?"

The service for Carter Aubery was basically a repeat of the one held for Hank Ullman, lacking something. Possibly it was the drabness of the museum itself. In the events of the last days its affairs had been neglected and when a donor reclaimed a work of art, an inferior piece took its place. Howard Stacey had even suggested bringing in the Mexican Army rifles from the defunct municipal museum. Michael Jarvits had been appalled.

Or it might have been the fact the bloom was off the memorial service itself. Two in so short a time invariably made the second anticlimactic. There were even audible yawns, during Gina's eulogy, a lengthy bore that made frequent mention of the Gutenberg Bible and the history of the printing press.

Finally it was over. Everyone sighed in relief.

Even the wine and delicacies that Gina trotted out appeared tasteless and flat.

"I'm not eating much," said Lars Waddington, catching Charlie's eye. "I'm looking forward to lunch."

Charlie smiled and turned to speak with Tod Van Spanckeren, whom he called earlier in the morning. He pulled him aside.

"A phone call—wasn't it?—that suggested narcotics were being played with?"

"You know it was."

Charlie gave a brief explanation of DLS. Tod Van Spanckeren listened, but was not too interested.

"Not necessary to tell me about DLS, Charlie. I've tried it."

"*You?*"

"Out at Mrs. Langley's. She said I had a creative brain. Or was it mind? Doesn't matter, I suppose. Anyway, I'm written up in the professional journals. What else?"

Charlie's information was non-committal, vague, but Tod accepted it readily. Almost as if it was what he wanted to hear. Charlie made no mention of Lorca or what he had discovered at the law office.

The restaurant Charlie had selected for lunch was some distance from Phoenix, in the locale of the Superstition Mountain, an establishment well-known for its "Prospector's Lunch."

Howard rode in the front seat with Charlie; Lars with Mrs. Crowley in the back. The old woman kept up a continual barrage of chatter, none of it making much sense.

"I told Gina I can fall down in the mud and come up with a man in each hand . . . I used to be on the stage, dancing and entertaining, not that movie thing. I hate movies. Like television. Nasty box, that's what it is ... My agent keeps calling me on the phone . . . they want me for the Albee circuit . . . I've got goddamn good legs. Go ahead, look at 'em, Howard. No sense of having gorgeous gams if they're not gonna be admired . . . Gina and her two husbands! *Bah*! I had three, but they were real men . . . Gina's gonna have the whole house done in Spanish Colonial ..."

Howard said the house had already been done in Spanish Colonial, but Mrs. Crowley babbled on, taking no notice.

"I'm going back in show business. Look at my legs, Howard."

An hour later they were at the restaurant on Apache Boulevard. In those sixty minutes, Mrs. Crowley had not once ceased to babble.

Stepping from the car, she said, "What is this place? What's that funny mountain?"

Lars said, "Superstition Mountain. Jacob Waltz. The Old Dutchman. Surely you know the legend of the Lost Dutchman Mine?"

"I knew him," gushed Mrs. Crowley. "One of my early admirers."

Miraculously, at lunch, Mrs. Crowley was subdued.

There was no menu and the food was served in gold-panning tins: steak, salad, hash browns, pinto beans and sourdough biscuits. Charlie and Mrs. Crowley had a cocktail. The other two declined.

"You're looking in condition, Howard. That day at the hospital I was really troubled. You were in rough shape."

"That's what everyone tells me. The next morning my sole sensation was that of hunger. I was famished. You'll have to forgive me, Charles, if I seemed out of sorts when you arrived. I appreciated your coming."

Charlie attacked his steak.

"Any more ideas about your friend with the stinger?"

"None. Had enough presence of mind to squash him on the instant. I recall that. And running for ice."

"Ice?"

"You should put ice on the sting immediately. I never should have run for the ice, though. That heated the blood. After I put on the ice, I called the doctor, and after that I was terribly sick. Remember nothing."

"Never been sick a day in my life," proclaimed Mrs. Crowley, who had pushed away her plate in favor of her cocktail.

"Mighty nice of you to invite us for lunch, Charlie."

"My pleasure, Lars. Everyone in Phoenix has been nice to me. It's the least I could do." He looked at both men and then at Mrs. Crowley. She was studying his movements with rigid interest. Her coolness disarmed him.

"I thought the service this morning was most dignified," Charlie lied.

"Yes, yes," Lars and Howard said in unison. Mrs. Crowley sipped her drink.

"But," began Charlie, and the three looked at him with expectation, "I found the museum rather – depressing."

Lars Waddington was a jovial man. Never in the brief time that Charlie had known him had he displayed anything but the most generous of emotions and attitudes.

"*If*," Lars began, and there was a malicious edge to that word, "the correct people served on the board, the museum would never be depressing. But never, I repeat – never is the artist consulted. Always, Charlie, it's the businessman, the moneyed man, the snobs who serve on such boards, while the artist must serve humanity and receive little, *if* anything, in return."

Charlie was dumbfounded.

Lars shot an angry glance at Howard, whose bland expression became a petulant pout.

"No," the museum's director declared in a voice of force, "the boards of museums should not include artists."

Lars turned on him in a fury.

"You're a hypocrite; you've been a frustrated artist all your life. Sublimating your urge in taxidermy! Don't attempt to fool yourself,

Howard. You may fool other people but not me, *not me*! Those that can, do; those who can't, teach."

Mrs. Crowley smiled knowingly.

"I'm thinking of returning to the stage. My agent called this morning. He wants to send me a new script. From a story by a young man. Somerset Maugham. It's called *Rain*."

They ignored her.

Howard Stacey came on strong with the counter-attack.

"*Artists*! What would any artist be without supervision? Van Gogh without his brother, yes, there's a good example."

"I'll wager it's the only example you'll be able to produce. You've been reading a book, Howard."

"I could give you other examples."

"Give me a half a dozen."

"You're acting like a madman. I have position at that museum."

"You said you're capable of other examples. I'd like to hear them, I would. Gina's is a museum devoted to the Fine Arts, Mr. Stacey, and the graphic arts, not a warehouse for army rifles from the Mexican Wars!"

Howard Stacey was the color of a beet.

Charlie had heard as much as he needed.

"Gentlemen, gentlemen," he soothed. "There's a lady present."

"Goddamn right," Mrs. Crowley agreed.

Lars Waddington ran his hand through his hair. "I – I apologize. I am most sensitive on this topic. I – I hope you'll forgive my outburst."

He appeared to be sincere.

Howard, too, calmed down. He said nothing else to Waddington and the burden of conversation fell to Charlie. Mrs. Crowley had suddenly become quite staid and proper.

By the time coffee had arrived, much, not all, of the tension had ebbed.

The ride back to Phoenix was painful because Mrs. Crowley didn't utter a single word.

Back at the museum they parted, the two men thanking Charlie profusely. Mrs. Crowley waved them on their way most regally.

"Where is your car, Mrs. Crowley?"

"Don't have one, Charlie."

"*What?*"

"I said I don't have one. They keep taking my license away. Even that Van Spanckeren man gave up. Couldn't get it back for me. I still drive. Don't tell Gina. How's that for a tune – 'Don't Tell Gina'?"

"Splendid. I have a friend who could do the lyrics."

"What now, Charles? You going to drive me back or am I going to hustle a cab?"

Charlie threw his arm around her and drew her close.

"No, you won't have to hustle a cab."

On their way to the house, Mrs. Crowley continued on in her previously talkative vein, exclaiming on her early days in show business. Hearts and flowers, until Charlie brought in the subject of Lorca.

Her mood changed.

". . . and after that, after the burial of Lorca, you and Mr. Jarvits never saw each other again?"

"Don't be an idiot. I saw him all the time."

"What I mean is – you never saw him to discuss what occurred that evening Dorothea smashed the car."

"No."

"Never talked to him about it?"

"I told you – no, except the next day."

"The next day?"

"When I called him at the museum."

"You called Mike Jarvits at the museum the day after Dorothea's death?"

"And told him Jerry had called and said Cinderella puffed up in smoke nice and neat, and I said I was going to put flowers around Lorca's grave. Better slow down, boy, you passed the gate to the house two minutes ago."

Chapter Fourteen

"Gina, how would you like to throw a dinner party?"

"That would depend entirely on who I had to invite. I presume, Charles, you'd furnish the guest list?"

"Only a part of it."

"Incidentally, Charles, I never *throw* dinner parties, I give them."

They were in the huge garage adjacent to the house. Charlie was talking to Gina as she bent over the motor of a Rolls Royce. She was becoming interested in mechanics, and had told an interviewer for *Practical Mechanics*, a few days earlier, that she was planning, temporarily, to abandon the arts for machinery.

Dolly sat in the front seat of a highly polished Mercedes Benz, the door open so she could hear the conversation.

Gina's words were muffled, because her head was low to the motor. She was garbed in mechanic's overalls, her hair in a multi-colored bandana, and even the grease smudges on her face fitted her new role.

"Will you do it?"

There was a dreadful clatter beneath the hood, followed by the sound of metal objects dropping.

Slowly Gina lifted her head from under the hood, looking perplexed. In her hand she held a wrench.

"I think," she said, "I've made a mistake somewhere."

"What's wrong with the motor?" Dolly asked.

"There's nothing wrong with it," replied Gina, "I merely want to find out how it functions. Since becoming increasingly interested in things mechanical, I thought working with the motor myself would give me excellent insight. Oh, dear, I think I twisted when I shouldn't have."

"Did you hurt yourself?" Dolly asked.

"Not me, Mrs. Underwood. I didn't twist anything on myself. The motor, Mrs. Underwood—something on the motor."

Dolly felt like a small child being reprimanded by an elder.

"Forgive me," said Dolly.

She imagined Gina bending over the motor, her rump ready for a swift kick. Dolly closed her eyes for an instant, enjoyed her fantasy and after she had delivered the mental boot, opened her eyes, relaxed and smiled.

Gina wiped at the grease smudges with a piece of tissue.

"A dinner party might be nice. Who did you want me to invite? We've had nothing but memorial services lately."

"You can invite whomever you wish, but there are some people I definitely want invited. More than that, I want them to come."

Head high, Gina replied imperviously, "When I invite someone to a dinner party at this house, Charles, they come."

Charlie cleared his throat.

"I'd like Howard Stacey and Lars Waddington."

"No problem there. Who else?"

"Tod Van Spanckeren."

"All right."

"Your mother, of course."

"Of course."

"Dolly and I will be there. Also, Michael Jarvits—"

"Delighted—"

"And Lisa Lynch."

Gina's expression soured.

"I heard a rumor that she was planning to return east. To leave Phoenix. Perhaps she won't be here for the party."

"Who told you that?"

"I don't remember. Must have been Mama. She's always saying things like that."

"You will invite her?"

"If you insist." She slammed down the hood of the car, none too gently, and proceeded to wipe her hands on a checkered cloth.

"I want to keep the gathering small, but I think it would look better if there were a few other people. Anyone you choose. No more than six."

"May I ask the reason for the party? Or isn't there one?"

She took a bottle of hand lotion from a work bench and began to work the oily cream into her hands.

"You're going on a trip, Gina."

The motion of the hands ceased.

"To the moon?" she smiled.

"I want this party to be a farewell party. Supposedly you'd be leaving a few days after it."

"If not the moon—where?"

"Doesn't matter. Any place you choose. Make it Spain."

"No, I dislike food fried in oil. Make it The Netherlands."

He smiled, "As you like."

The hand massaging continued.

"I'm not really going anywhere, am I?"

"Let's say – not far."

"When will this dinner party take place?"

"Day after tomorrow."

"That soon? Is that all there is to it?"

"No, I want you to call a press conference. Today, if possible."

"It's possible. And what am I to say?"

Charlie leaned against the bumper of the Rolls Royce. "You said you'd trust me. I prefer you didn't ask too many questions."

"Just as I'm told, is that it?"

"That's it."

She affected a grin, "You sound masterful, Charlie. Under other circumstances that would be appealing. I have no choice, do I? After what you discovered about Lorca and that – that girl. We'll all have to wade through. In you we trust."

"You *do* trust me?"

Gina Langley took a pack of cigarettes from her pocket, spurning Charlie's offer of a match. She took a deep drag and let the smoke pass through her lips slowly in a steady stream.

"Charles, never in my life have I ever trusted anyone. Especially a man."

They drove back to Mountain Shadows slowly, taking in the quiet majesty of a cool desert day.

"I have to admire her," said Dolly. "I don't like her, not actually. God knows she's chilly to me. I can mark that down to her dislike of women generally and I must say I am not impressed with the range of her activities. Anyone else who flitted from thing to thing would be considered a restless person."

"That's something of a silly thing to say, Dolly."

"How so?"

"Naturally, she's restless. More than that, she's bored. Gina Langley is a twentieth-century hetaera. She has been right at home in the Italian Renaissance, maintaining a salon for painters and writers. She has the mind of a man in the body of a woman. She thinks like a man—"

Dolly made a sound indicating she didn't go along with the analysis.

"Okay, but I believe what I'm saying is correct, Dolly. You said you admired her."

"Any woman who's accomplished as much as Gina deserves admiration. So I'm envious. What did you make of her reaction to your asking that Lisa be invited to the dinner party?"

"Don't know. More than I bargained for."

Dolly rested her head on the back of the seat.

"What is having Gina close the museum going to prove?"

"Who murdered Ullman and Carter, who poisoned Howard, and tried to do the same with me."

He looked at his wristwatch.

"If she did as I told her, that press conference is about to begin."

In their cabana, the Underwoods continued to discuss various details of the case. Charlie recalled the heated exchange between Howard Stacey and Lars Waddington.

Dolly was seated on the edge of the double bed (the Underwoods abhorred single beds), stripping off her hose. Charlie was in the bathroom, showering.

Stockings off, Dolly entered the bathroom and stood by the door. The shower stall was low enough to carry on conversation, although the volume of the voice had to be high.

"Lars and Howard, that's interesting. Lars impressed me as such a quiet chap. Hey, know something, Charlie? That day we went out to look at his new paintings--?"

"I remember."

"He was going to show us three. We only saw one."

"Smart girl."

"What ever happened to the birds?"

"The birds?"

Exasperatedly, she said, "The ones in the cages."

"Oh, *those*. Old lady Crowley said Gina donated them to the zoo."

Girlishly, Dolly said, "What are we doing tonight, sweetheart?"

"We're going to have dinner here."

"In the room?"

"No, the terrace room. Call up Lisa and tell her it's important. Invite her. Say about seven."

"What if I can't get them?"

"*Them?*"

"Lisa and Mike."

He turned the faucet and the rush of water stopped. He put his two hands on the top sill of the shower door.

"Dolly, I don't want you to invite Mike Jarvits. Lisa. *Solo*."

"Why? It's not polite to invite her without—"

The look in Charlie's eyes ended the discussion.

The Terrace Dining Room, something like Carter Aubery's apartment, was surrounded on four sides by an unbroken sheet of curved window. The effect of the desert encompassing the setting was exceptionally dazzling.

Dinner was good and Lisa ate hungrily.

"Fish," she said, in appreciation of her lobster, "is not easy to come by here on the desert. I mean *fresh* fish. What there is is flown from the Gulf of Guaymas or from the Coast. I love lobsters, but most of all I love their claws. That's the trouble with lobsters that don't come from the East—no claws. But this is delicious—I'll have to say that."

Charlie said, "I'm told Gina Langley is going to have a dinner party in a day or so."

Lisa poked a piece of lobster, held her fork in mid-air before bringing it to her mouth.

"She's always having them. I understand she does them well. That's what Mike says."

"You've never been to a dinner party at the house?"

She was embarrassed. Dolly was sorry for her.

"Why—why, no. As a matter of fact, I haven't."

"She doesn't like women too much," Dolly smiled, hoping to ease her friend's predicament.

"She has no objection if they're elderly and look it. No competition, I guess you could say."

"Have you seen Howard Stacey recently?"

"No, not at all. I imagine he's carrying on a struggle with the blank walls at the museum. You'd think people would have let the museum keep their paintings just a shade longer. But Gina Langley is a scatterbrain. Oh, wealthy, healthy and wise, I suppose. But I've never been confident the woman's one hundred percent sane."

"Who is?" asked Charlie.

"You impress me as being sane, Charlie. You and Dolly are the two sanest people I know."

"You've never seen us on anything but our best behavior."

"I'm afraid I don't understand."

"Another one of my theories about life and about people. My old man was something of a theorist. In the woods of New Hampshire."

"Woods?"

Dolly explained: "Charlie's father was in lumber."

"Oh," said Miss Lynch, not understanding any more than she did before the explanation.

"As I was saying, you've seen us on our best behavior. Have you ever seen me, the person you're positive is sane, under duress? Tension? Pushed to a breaking point?"

Lisa was unhappy with the trend of conversation.

"Or Dolly? What about your dancing friend, Dolly Adrian?"

"She always made me think she was sane. When we were dancing in shows, when we were both younger, Dolly had her head on her shoulders. Yes, always. I was the one getting into the strange situations. I tell myself it was because I was younger. I wanted to experience—"

"Experience—"

Lisa cast her eyes downward.

"Experience life." She smiled, rather girlishly.

"What will you do now that Gina is closing the museum?"

The sentence had been asked in a monotone and it took a second or two for its import to sink in. When it did, Lisa managed to knock over her wine glass, the ruby liquid soaking into the thick white tablecloth like a silent accuser.

"How clumsy of me," Lisa said and she brought her glass back to a standing position. A busboy quickly spread a napkin over the red spot, and stepped away.

"What – what do you mean? Close the museum?"

"Haven't you heard? Hasn't Mike told you? She wants to think about the future of the museum. Turned out to be more of an undertaking than she anticipated and now with Carter gone and Ullman and Miss Darnell and Jerry—"

Lisa pinched at the stem of her wine glass.

"Jerry? Who's that?"

"Mike's friend, Jerry Cox."

Lisa swallowed some water in tiny, noisy gulps.

"I – I don't know the man."

"Oh? I thought you did. Didn't mean to break the news this way. I thought you knew. What I was wondering is – is Gina going to keep Mike on the payroll even though the place is shuttered--?"

"I don't know."

"Or is she going to take his advice and turn it over to the city?"

"To the city?"

"Isn't that what Mike's been suggesting to her? I had the impression one reason the city was so lenient on taxes, land assessments, etcetera, was because it expected the place would be turned over in a reasonable length of time. Wasn't that it? Isn't that the reason the city closed that relic they had and haven't started any plans of their own?"

To both Charlie and Dolly it seemed as if a veil had suddenly drifted over Lisa's face. A moment ago when Charlie began to question Lisa, she was scared. It was written on her face; now her facial muscles relaxed and she smiled.

"You – you threw me, Charlie. On top of everything else, I had no warning of this action on Gina Langley's part."

"Mike was planning on leaving for the East anyway, wasn't he?"

"He talked about it. I may have mentioned to Dolly about Mike resigning. Even if he did, he'd have to stay on for a month or so to tie up some loose ends. What I told Dolly was in the strictest confidence, Charlie. I had no idea the matter would get bandied about."

Lisa looked accusingly at Dolly. Charlie's wife felt guilty and uncomfortable.

"Is he?"

Lisa was infuriated, but kept her anger under control.

"Is he *what*?"

"Resigning."

"He's talked about it. You'll have to ask him if you wish to be positive."

The waiter brought dessert menus. Dolly had a tortino. Charlie passed up dessert in favor of brandy. Lisa had neither.

"I think I'd like to head back into town," said Lisa abruptly. "I'd like to see Mike before he turns in."

Over Dolly's protests, Lisa rose from the table, plainly out of sorts, mumbled thank you and goodbye, and started on her way. What had begun pleasantly enough had ended on a note of tension.

Dolly stabbed at her dessert with a tiny silver spoon.

"You gave that girl a hard time, Charlie, and I didn't like it. Why the Gestapo tactics? The bearing down?"

"Had some results, didn't it?"

"*What* results? Tell me that."

"She didn't know about Gina closing the museum."

Dolly put down the spoon.

"For goodness sake – who does? I thought no one would know until morning."

"You will admit she was disturbed."

Dolly was annoyed.

"*Men*," she said through her clenched teeth, "you invite the girl to dinner. Supposedly for a nice evening with friends. You know she's terribly upset about Mike and what do you do? You needle her."

He said nothing. A thin, not unkind, smile was on his lips. He could have been holding back a laugh.

"All right, dear, why do you think she got so rattled? You believe what happened with the wine glass was a normal reaction?"

"Yes, I do. To the point, Mike hasn't been what you call open with Lisa. As far as we know, the poor girl doesn't even know about

Mike's affair with Dorothea. Worse, though -- she suspects. She tells me about Mike planning to quit in the utmost secrecy, she thinks, and you run off at the mouth about it. Certainly she's confused and upset. Who can she trust?"

Charlie tried to get in a word, but Dolly would have none of it.

"On top of everything else you announce, casually in that famous Underwood manner, that Gina Langley is closing the museum. Don't you think Lisa feels that she should have heard that from Mike first? If Mike doesn't tell her things like that, if he keeps holding things back – where precisely does Lisa stand in his life? Damn right she was irritable and nervous. What woman under similar circumstances would act otherwise?"

"You, Dolly, are speaking from the woman's point of view."

"What did you hope to prove by teasing her?"

He sipped his brandy.

"Sweetheart. I'm checking out everyone. If I ruffle enough feathers maybe we'll see our bird. That's why I had lunch with three suspects after Aubery's memorial service. One by one, I'm needling them. I admit it. To make an omelet you have to scramble some eggs."

"That's not how it goes. Break some eggs to make an omelet."

"You're so smart, Dolly. I guess that's why I married you."

"All this provoking and all, is it going to pay off?"

"I hope so. At the farewell party."

After dinner they walked along the terrace in silence, Charlie lost in concentration, wondering if what Dolly surmised might not be correct after all: Lisa's reactions were normal and proved nothing.

By the same logic, Howard and Lars going at each other might be the result of nerves worn thin. No doubt about it, everything was coming to a head. The vision of a guillotine crossed Charlie's thoughts.

"Come on, Dolly," he said, troubled, taking his wife by the arm. "Let's turn in early tonight."

"There is one thing. Something Gina said this morning in the garage. About our guest tonight."

"I don't recall."

"She said she heard a rumor Lisa might be heading east, leaving Phoenix."

"That's right. Wonder who she heard that from?"

"I've a vague idea. Time will tell."

By the time they reached the cabana door, Lisa Lynch's sports car, silvery in the moonlight, had already entered Gina Langley's driveway.

Chapter Fifteen

All the morning papers carried, basically, the same story. In the *Journal*, with no byline:

> Gina Langley, well-known Valley socialite, authoress, film actress and patron of the arts, announced at a press conference late yesterday afternoon, that she is closing the recently opened Langley Memorial Art Museum, named in memory of her late husband, Osbert. Mrs. Langley reached her decision, she said, after considerable thought.
>
> "I opened the museum much too soon. What makes a museum is not the outer shell, but what is contained within."
>
> The announcement came as a shock to the area's art lovers. Mrs. Langley will leave shortly for Europe. No plans for the building have been announced. Board members were not available for comment. The museum has been open less than a week. (See Museum, Entertainment Section.)

"You didn't have to read it to me," said Charlie. "I practically wrote the whole damn thing."

Tod Van Spanckeren was not pleased.

"I thought we were going to work on this case together."

"I think we are."

"I've heard of rivalry between professional policemen – notice I didn't say cop and private investigators."

"You don't think much of my plans?"

Tod was seated. He picked up a pencil and brandished it threateningly, as he was prone to do when angry.

"I didn't say that. As a matter of fact it sounds plausible. Damn plausible. What I object is the way you've shot off on this tangent and come here to me after it's set to roll."

Charlie stretched out his legs.

"I had a reason."

"I hope so. A good one."

The policeman calmed down, his annoyance checked.

"I can afford to play hunches, Tod. You can't. If I make a mistake, no problem. With you, on the other hand – it could mean your job."

"Go on."

"Suppose I came to you and told you why I thought murder had been committed, and why I thought I knew the murderer, and why I thought my plan to catch the murderer would work – what would your reaction be?"

"Considering your plan, I'd say the guy who thought of it was fairly clever."

"Do you believe I'm right?"

"I think everything you've said, every step of the way, sounds clear and logical. But there's one thing my policeman's brain rebels at."

"What's that?"

"You haven't a shred of evidence."

"I don't deny it. Evidence that you'd consider solid, that is. Again, that's where I have the advantage over you."

Tod pushed at the newspaper.

"Closing the museum. A wild stab."

"Not too wild. Sort of thing Gina would do."

"Perhaps. Says here the board couldn't be reached."

"What's left of the board."

"The dinner party thing, you actually think it'll work?"

"I do. Word is out that Gina plans to spend the next two years traveling. She'll leave the morning after the party."

"And if your suspect doesn't make the play, then what?"

Charlie forced a reluctant smile.

"I hadn't thought about it."

"You put all your eggs in one basket, don't you?"

"I try not to, but sometimes it can't be avoided."

Tod lifted himself from the chair with a push, came around to the front of his desk and sat on the edge.

"Charlie, you've found out quite a bit about these people. What I term 'my charges.' I've listened, and for part of the way, I'm with you."

"Thanks."

The policeman was angling for something, this Charlie could sense.

"In everything you've told me – let's start with the Ullman death – I admit your idea on how he might have been whacked is good. But it's not good enough. There's no proof whatsoever, consequently, as far as the police department is concerned. Henry Ullman met his death by accident. Let's pass him by. Howard Stacey insists that all the scorpions in his jar were dead. He was stung by a live one, this we know. However, it is entirely possible that Howard was mistaken when he put the things in the jar. They weren't in formaldehyde or any preservative. Stacey may have been stung because of his own carelessness. We come to Carter Aubery—"

"Ah," said Charlie with delight, "but it was you who pointed out the lack of hesitation marks on his wrists."

"Even here, Charles, there is nothing conclusive. Be difficult to make that observation stand as evidence of murder. Carter Aubery may have been the exception to the rule. Exceptions exist. Might even have been under sedation or intoxicated, which, according to the lab tests, he *was*. You get my point – nowhere is there any proof, unless—"

"Unless it turns up at the dinner party."

Tod smiled, "We can always hope. No, I wasn't thinking about the dinner party. I was thinking – hard proof, irrefutably."

"Like what?"

"Oh, I don't know. A corpse is always irrefutable. How about Dorothea Darnell? In all your investigating what have you found out about her disappearance?"

Charlie was mentally squirming.

"Yeah, Dorothea, well – to tell the truth—"

"The truth is always the best course."

"Always?"

"How do you mean that?"

"From what I gathered, everyone concerned with that gal would be better off without her, wouldn't you say?"

"Not important what I'd say. What interests me is what you're saying."

"Suppose Dorothea went away—"

"Like Jerry Cox?"

There was an interval of silence.

Charlie's composure slipped: "*Jerry Cox?*"

Tod smiled, went once again behind his desk and picked up a folder, opening it as he did so.

"You haven't met Mr. Cox?"

Charlie said nothing.

"My error, I thought you had. An uninteresting type. This file gives his several names. Engaged in sundry annoyances – signing his name to the wrong check. Petty stuff."

"You've talked with this Cox?"

"I *told* you, Charles, Gina Langley and her mother are something of my business. I watch everyone that comes in contact with them. Some people, *bad* people," he said this wryly, "might even attempt blackmail. I like to keep an eye on people who have business dealings with those women. You know how they are. When a man like Hank Ullman's partner, Jenckes, tells me a check has come through – a thousand dollars – for the cremation of one dog, and made out to Mr. Cox, I get to wondering, know what I mean? Nutty as old lady Crowley is, her checks do not bounce."

"I wouldn't know," said Charles, his calm returning. "The one she gave me wasn't signed."

"What would you make of a check for one thousand dollars to an attendant at a pet cemetery?"

Charlie thought, then said, "Not too much, if I truly had the old woman's interest at heart. Suppose, let's guess here, a woman like Dorothea Darnell died in an automobile accident. Let's say she was drunk, let's say dangerous. Behind a wheel she might even run down a dog. Kill the animal. Let's say there's an old lady, batty but clear-headed now and again, and maybe she thinks it would be a terrible thing for any publicity to get out about the death, especially if the woman in the car had been drinking or swallowed too many unusual pills.

"Maybe, too, there's a man who says he'll help her get rid of the body, so there'll be no ugly scandal—who suffers? You could always put away the old lady, I guess. Arrest the young man who helped her out." He paused before continuing to gauge Ted's reaction. The policeman was listening intently.

"Amazing," said Charlie brightly, "the paths guesswork takes you on."

Van Spanckeren's reply: "In some circumstances."

Charlie had tripped himself and he knew Van Spanckeren saw him do it. He had underestimated the policeman. Tod knew far more than Charlie had suspected. The revelation was both comforting and unnerving, depending entirely on how the policeman would decide to play the game. Charlie waited. Tod continued to study the folder. He put it down and took another.

"Yes, quite a woman," he said.

"Mrs. Crowley?"

"Hair black as ebony, skin white as snow. No, this file is on Miss Darnell." Softly he said, "Yes, indeed, quite a girl. I suppose in one sense the world would be a far better place without women like her, but respect for the law makes the world a better place."

Charlie said, "This – this Cox person is wanted for something?"

Van Spanckeren put down the Darnell folder and turned his attention to Cox's.

"Absolutely nothing. His record at the moment is clear. But he *has* a record."

In a swift gesture he slammed flat the thin cover of the folder.

"I don't have much choice, do I? About the dinner party?"

"I'm confident it will work."

The policeman's manner was direct.

"For your sake, Underwood, as much as Jerry Cox's, it'd better."

Late the following afternoon, the Valley experienced a tremendous rain. The skies opened and poured down a continuous gush. Dusty roads were transformed into muddy avenues and in several places the water had caused flooding.

The Underwoods were ready to leave their cabana at Mountain Shadows. Charlie was somewhat out of sorts. Gina Langley had gone along with his every wish; indeed, she had taken to the idea of the dinner party like a restless child to imaginative play. Engraved invitations had been personally delivered and to Charlie's chagrin he discovered that the affair was black tie.

He fumbled with his tie.

"For goodness sake, Charlie, relax. Simply because Gina wants a formal dinner party is no reason for you to get fidgety."

"Great for you dames—"

"I'm not a dame, dear."

"I had to rent this damn thing."

Dolly sat before her dressing mirror catching glimpses of Charlie in the mirror. He looked unusually handsome in his formal evening suit.

He said, "I never feel comfortable when I have to dress like this."

She replied, "That's because you were brought up in the backwoods of New Hampshire."

He finished tying his tie.

"You make it sound like Okefenokee, or the hills of West Virginia. Lumber forests and backwoods are not the same thing, and I'll have you know, wife, that when I attended Exeter I was often – I repeat – often attired thusly."

"My, aren't we feeling literate this evening."

She turned and faced Charlie. He was standing.

"How do I look, darling?"

She stood, also, and modeled her outfit.

Dolly had been delighted when the invitation arrived. Perhaps ecstatic would be a better word. She, also like Charlie, had assumed the dinner party would be a small gathering in spite of its intent, informal and relaxed. Since they had arrived in the Valley of the Sun she had slight opportunity to dress in anything but sports clothes and swimsuits, but now--!

Minutes after the invitation had arrived she was in the Fashionette Shoppe of the hotel, surrounded by salesgirls and a seamstress. She selected a white, pearl-trimmed gown cut in Empire fashion with a pale damask Skinner satin opera coat.

She didn't quote Charlie the price. He'd find it on the hotel bill at checkout. On pins and needles she had waited, until shortly before five, when the seamstress, breathless, but happy and excited, delivered the gown.

Under ordinary circumstances the dress would not have been selected because Dolly was cautious of white with her blonde hair, but this was an off-white that gave a golden tone to her tanned skin, making the lightness of her hair fit the scheme radiantly.

"Darling, I'm waiting for an appraisal."

Charlie gave a long, low whistle and took her in his arms.

"Why do I love you?" he asked, kissing her.

Throatily, she answered, "Because I look so good in this gown and this opera coat. I do, don't I, Charlie?"

"Yes, yes," he replied slowly, massaging her back with his hand and enjoying it tremendously.

Cleverly, Dolly maneuvered, "Then you won't object to the price."

"'Course not," he said, pressing closer. "How much was it?"

Kittenishly, she asked, "Everything included?"

His reply was a sensual grunt.

"Two hundred and sixty-one dollars."

He stopped the massage, stepped back and stared in disbelief.

"*What!*"

"Charlie, Charlie, there may be photographers there. After all, this *is* a Gina Langley party. You wouldn't want your wife to go there dressed in the best Montgomery and Ward had to offer."

He was thinking of something to say, something along the lines of – "This dinner party is not a dinner party; it's a ruse to catch a killer; it an attempt to solve—"

The telephone rang and Dolly lifted the receiver.

"Yes, Lisa . . . you'll be a trifle late? . . . fine . . . yes, Lisa, I'll tell Charlie—"

Charlie made a sign that she shouldn't hang up.

Dolly put her hand over the mouthpiece and said, "Howard's car wouldn't start, so Lisa and Mike will pick him up at his house and drive him to Gina's."

"Okay," he answered. "Ask her if she's talked with anyone else today, or if there's been any new phone calls."

She asked.

Again, she covered the mouthpiece. "She says there've been no phone calls that she knows about and the only person she's talked to in person was Tod Van Spanckeren. Mrs. Crowley called, too, to make certain Lisa was coming, but that's not what you meant by a phone call, is it?"

Charlie found this interesting and nodded that he had all the information he wanted from Lisa. For the moment.

When Lisa rang off, Charlie went to the phone, dialed a number and waited impatiently.

"Van Spanckeren?"

The voice at the other end answered, a conversation ensued. Dolly listened, intrigued. She forgot about her loveliness for a moment. Charlie finished giving his instructions to the policeman and said goodbye.

"What was that about?" she asked.

"You'll find out later, I hope. Come on, Snow White, the mirror says you're the fairest in the land."

She turned toward him. "Don't call me 'Snow White,' dear. Unpleasant connotations. Besides it wasn't Snow White who questioned the mirror. It was a wicked queen or witch or someone along those lines."

She gave herself one final appraisal in the mirror.

"I'm ready."

"Let's go."

At the door, she paused.

"Be careful, Charlie, tonight. Promise me."

"I'm not worried about taking care of myself, Dolly, but I am about taking care of Gina Langley. If I've guessed wrong, that museum will have one more murder in its log."

Before she could make a reply, Charlie turned up the collar of his raincoat, helped Dolly arrange a plastic one over her frock coat and closed the door.

Thunder.

The ride to Gina's took much longer than Charlie expected. The weather was vile. He had to inch along cautiously. Even his car lights on highest beam barely cut the curtain of rain.

The house was aglow with candle illumination. The guests all seemed to be arriving at the same time, for there was a car ahead of the Underwoods and one following.

The first car had two people, a man and a woman. A servant

waited with a mushroom of an umbrella. As soon as they were out of the car, a young Mexican boy slid into the driver's seat and drove the car off in the direction of the garages.

The procedure was repeated for the Underwoods and the third car, which contained two men and a woman.

People were clustered in the entry hall, shaking their clothes of rain.

A maid took umbrellas, raincoats, hats, and Juan—the butler the Underwoods had come to recognize—showed the way to their hostess. The man last to arrive in the entry hall took off his raincoat and laid it atop the others. The maid smiled for a greeting. In handing her his own raincoat, he helped her with the others. One raincoat weighed heavily. He saw an object protruding from the pocket, its metallic hardness evident. It was the handle of a .38.

The man swallowed hard, pushed the revolver back into the pocket of the raincoat and handed it to the maid, who had seen the weapon, but made no comment. Having worked for Gina Langley over a period of five years, nothing would have surprised her.

In the living room, not one electric bulb was in evidence. Candles everywhere. Gina was talking to an elderly woman.

"Mrs. Underwood," she exclaimed with admiration, "you look stunning. *Stunning.*"

Mrs. Langley could afford to be generous with her compliments. Apart from herself there were five other women present. Her mother, Mrs. Crowley, was draped in a purple sheath that fitted her bony body like a wrinkled glove. She fit in well with the candles. A tiara crowned her white hair, on every finger save the thumbs sparkled ornamentation. She had affected gem-trimmed dark glasses.

Lisa had chosen to wear a knee-length evening dress; Mrs. Jenckes, the lawyer's wife, had also, while the woman Gina had been conversing with was in a hostess gown inspired by some bygone era. With each woman, jewelry played an important part in the costuming. Gina, however, had chosen a gown of shimmering silk, pale blue. She wore not a single piece of jewelry, and the effect was both compelling and dramatic.

"This," Gina said proudly, "is Mr. and Mrs. Conforth. Cynthia and Leonard." They exchanged greetings with the Underwoods.

The man had a long, coffin-like face; the woman was homely and displayed teeth that were discolored and wide set.

"Mr. and Mrs. Conforth are delegates from the Mondcivitan Republic."

Dolly feigned admiration, although she was correct in assuming she had never heard of any such country. Charlie was puzzled, too.

Gina explained. "A Commonwealth of World Citizens. They have a capital somewhere in Yugoslavia, I believe."

"No, no," corrected Mrs. Conforth. "Not Yugoslavia—Great Britain."

"I thought it was Yugoslavia," said Gina. "Sounds very Merry Widowish to me."

Cynthia Conforth did not care for the implication.

She held an extremely long cigarette holder in one hand and a cocktail in another.

"No, no, Gina, you persist in fostering the wrong attitude. In our time a new nation without territory of its own had come into existence, the Commonwealth of World Citizens ..."

"How pleasant," said Gina. "For you."

Cynthia lifted one eyebrow archly. She looked wicked.

"Gina, these two young people may be interested. You *are* interested, aren't you?"

"Yes," Charlie and Dolly lied in unison.

A maid passed with a tray of cocktails. Charlie selected one for Dolly, a martini, and one for himself, bourbon on the rocks. Everyone he wanted to be present, was.

"As I was saying, a Commonwealth of World Citizens organized under its own government as the Mondcivitan Republic. Mondcivitan is from the Esperanto for World Citizen, you see. Leonard here has an ambassadorial rank—"

Surreptitiously, Charlie edged away, leaving Dolly trapped with the

diplomats. He nodded at Tod Van Spanckeren, but by pre-arrange-
ment they didn't converse. Lisa, Howard, and Mike were seated on
a long low sofa, Mrs. Crowley in a chair nearby. At the moment, she
appeared sane, despite the outlandishness of her clothes.

Charlie sat on the arm of the sofa.

"Make it through the mud with no trouble?"

"Not much trouble," answered Mike. "The road to Howard's is
well paved. Dirt roads make for the trouble."

"Don't have to tell me," Charlie said. "I've been through them."

"Hated to put Mike and Lisa to trouble here, but my automobile
wouldn't start. I believe it's the battery. Every time it rains I have
trouble with the battery. Gina's called a rental agency for me. They're
sending out a car."

"You shouldn't have done that, Howard," said Lisa.

"I'll need a car in the morning, anyway. Terrible inconvenience for
you to pick me up as it was—"

Lisa started to protest.

Howard shook his head. "Car will be here before dinner."

Lisa sighed, "I'm hopeless when it comes to motors and things
like that. The other evening when I drove in here to get Mike, the car
stalled several times. I thought I'd be stuck on the road. I wouldn't
know what to do."

"When was that?" Mike asked.

"A couple of nights ago. The evening I had dinner with Charlie
and Dolly at the Shadows. Remember – you were having some meeting here at the house."

"Oh, I remember, but it's strange," he said, "the car never stalls
when I drive it. Woman driver, that's what."

She nudged him playfully.

"How are you feeling, Howard?"

"Charles, to be honest, not too good. If it wasn't for this party
– I mean if it wasn't *Gina's* party – I don't believe I would have attended."

"More reaction from the sting?"

"Getting old, more likely."

The gathering laughed self-consciously. All, except Mrs. Crowley.

"You want to be an old goat, be an old goat. Don't have to be if you don't want to be. Look at me! Look at Gina, betcha my daughter's older than you, Howard Stacey. Don't hear her complaining about pains and aches."

"I'm not complaining about aches and pains, Mrs. Crowley."

"You are, too, I heard. Don't lie."

In the forty-five minutes before dinner was announced, Charlie was able to keep track of the men who left the room. Dolly's assignment was to keep track of the women. Lars Waddington, who had remained aloof, left twice. Mr. Jenckes once, Michael Jarvits once. On the female side, Mrs. Crowley had absented herself for approximately twenty minutes.

Charlie managed to speak to most of the people in the room. With Lars conversation had been limited. The artist said he wasn't himself because of a new painting. (It was going badly.) Every time Charlie passed Cynthia Conforth she was continuing with her lecture. Dolly was trapped.

"Relations between Mondcivitans of all races are those of kinship and common nationality ..."

The woman was impossible; Charlie hoped he wasn't placed beside her at dinner.

"Dinner is served," announced Juan in his deep, booming voice.

"'bout time," bellowed Mrs. Crowley. "I'm hungry!"

Everyone pretended they hadn't heard her.

Walking into the dining room, Mike Jarvits felt the clawing hand of Mrs. Crowley grasp his wrist. She pulled him aside.

"Gina wants you to see her, when everyone is gone. You come to the library alone. It's important."

"When everyone is gone?"

"Are you deaf? Do as I tell you, young man, see me when everyone is gone."

"I thought you said Gina."

His attempt at clarification failed. Mrs. Crowley skipped ahead and slipped her arm in Tod Van Spanckeren's. She entered the dining room like an Empress.

At table, Charlie suddenly was seized with a wave of doubt. What if plans failed? He looked across the table at Tod, hoping for a sign, but the policeman was trapped by a World Citizen, expounding of passport difficulties encountered by Mondcivitans.

Everything was moving according to plan, but there's a nagging doubt which persisted. What if a miscalculation had been made? What if the killer would decide not to go through with it? What . . .?

Conversation was lively from time to time. That is, when Gina allowed others the opportunity of speaking.

She talked at length about her proposed trip.

"In the morning, I'll be on my way. Like a butterfly, flitting to The Hague."

"You must drop in at headquarters," volunteered Mr. Conforth. (His sole comment at dinner.)

Only Mrs. Conforth was unthinking enough to ask, "What happens to everyone at the museum?"

Lars Waddington replied, "If you mean *artists*, we will continue to paint."

"No, not artists," said Cynthia Conforth, "the employees?"

"I shall have to think about that," said Gina.

Her tone was frosty. Mrs. Jenckes had been about to ask something else, but changed her mind. She continued eating in silence.

"Where's she going?" inquired Mrs. Crowley of Tod. "Gina's going somewhere?"

"Your daughter's going to Europe."

"Where?"

"Europe."

"When?"

"In the morning."

"But she's having the whole house done over in Spanish Colonial. Can't have the whole house done over in Spanish Colonial if she's going to Europe in the morning."

Gina placed her napkin beside her plate and stood, commanding, "Shall we have coffee in the living room?"

The guests rose, noiselessly, and filed after their hostess, leaving Mrs. Crowley seated at her place, gleefully spooning her dessert. A parfait.

Russian cigarettes, pre-Castro Cuban cigars and brandy were passed on trays. One by one, the guests expressed their sadness at Gina's departure. Lars asked her to reconsider about the museum and she had laughed gaily, which annoyed him.

"All my affairs are in the hands of Mr. Jenckes," she said with a wave of her hand, as if this gesture, coupled with her remark, would take care of any and all problems.

The first to leave was Howard Stacey, who apologized, holding his recent illness as his excuse. Gina promised to call him in the morning and he left, followed in short order by the Jenckses, Waddington, Conforths. Tod bade goodnight and told Gina he would see her to the airport in the morning.

When the Underwoods said goodnight, Lisa and Mike were directly behind them.

Regally, Gina held out her hand and Mike held it for a moment.

"I will see you before I leave," she said.

Mike was confused. Did this mean Mrs. Crowley had meant what she said – that he was to return to the house alone? Or was Mrs. Crowley rattled as usual? Did Gina mean tonight or in the morning?

The rain had stopped, but a drizzle continued. The friends departed, with goodnights. The car attendant swung Charlie's car into the driveway and the Underwoods got in and drove off, waving goodbye.

Lisa turned to Michael. "I got the impression Gina wanted to speak to you. Now. Did you?"

"I don't know. Listen, honey, wait in the car. I'll see her for a moment. This won't take long."

Lisa did as she was asked, pulling the car forward in the drive.

Mike rapped on the medieval knocker Gina fancied.

Juan opened the door.

"I'd like to see Mrs. Langley."

"In the library, Mr. Jarvits."

The door to the library was open. Lights were on in the room. Electric ones. The drapes at the far end of the room that covered the French doors were drawn wide apart and the sky visible was blackly ominous.

"Ah, Mike. The door, close the door please."

Her voice traveled the long length of the gallery room and in doing so, sounded muted and remote.

Walking toward her he said, "Did I understand your mother correctly?"

"My mother?"

"When she said you wanted to see me after the others had gone?"

"How strange. I mean, that she should have said that."

"You did want to see me?"

"Why, no, Mike, I thought it was you who wanted to see me. Haven't you come back to tell me something?"

"No, I haven't."

"I thought you had returned to reproach me."

"Why would I want to do that?"

"You should know the answer to that."

This was unlike Gina, not to offer him a chair, but she didn't. She was braced with her back against the French doors.

"Yes, Michael," she said, "you, above all people, should know the answer to that. You're angry because I haven't followed your advice about signing the museum over to the city."

"I'm not in the least angry, Gina. That's entirely your decision. I recommended the step—"

"And you're angry because of Dorothea—"

"I'm not angry about her—"

"And you have no position with the museum now. You're out of work. That angers you."

He laughed, not unkindly.

"Gina, what is this? You gave me a fantastic bonus to come to Phoenix. I planned to leave anyway, and now that you've de-cided—"

She was pacing again. In her hand she held a chiffon handkerchief and he noticed that she was twisting it into a knot. Her words, too, were stagy, over-articulated.

"Pour the chocolate," she said, indicating the pot and cups on a small table. He moved toward the stand and bent over the silver pot, saying: "Is something wrong, Gina? You're so—"

Before he could finish his sentence a shot rang out. In a fraction of a second it had happened. Too fast to comprehend. Then another shot. And another. He was on the floor, flattened out. The sound of running feet was heard outside in the inner patio and the frantic voices of men shouting things he couldn't decipher.

Shortly thereafter, there was pounding on the door of the library and the sound of the butler's voice, imploring. The door opened and Charlie and Dolly rushed in. Lisa Lynch and Juan were close behind.

Uneasy, shaken, Michael Jarvits pulled himself from the floor.

Their eyes looked at him accusingly. The revolver was close to where he had lain. He watched them look at it. His eyes traveled to where Gina Langley had fallen.

Michael Jarvits found the woman lovely still, even in death.

"Oh, my God, Gina," he sobbed in disbelief. "Oh, my God."

Chapter Sixteen

"To begin with," said Charlie, "anyone who knows Gina and her habits is aware that every evening she comes in here, this room, reads some, drinks hot chocolate. She thinks of it as her quiet hour."

"What made him so positive that I'd come in, too?" asked Mike.

"He wasn't. Not entirely." Charlie looked in the direction of Mrs. Crowley. She had fallen asleep in a high-back chair. "He told Mrs. Crowley to tell you Gina wished to see you here after the others had left."

Mike insisted: "But what if I hadn't returned?"

"I suppose then he'd make the attempt early this morning. You'd be home asleep, not a good alibi, you'll admit. Luck was with him, however. Mrs. Crowley got the message straight."

Dolly interjected: "Mrs. Crowley would be able to identify him as the man who gave her the message. Wouldn't she?"

Charlie stole a nervous glance to his sleeper. "Maybe yes, maybe no. After a length of time—a short length—Mrs. Crowley gets rather confused about who said what. When he left the gathering tonight, he was able to take the revolver from Mike's raincoat without the maid seeing him. Let's not forget, though, that the maid had seen the revolver earlier in the evening. He had stacked the raincoats for her and made sure the weapon protruded from Mike's pocket."

"And," said Mike, following the deduction, "when I went to get my raincoat I wouldn't notice anything out of line since I didn't know the gun had been put into the coat in the first place."

"Right. Wasn't there when you drove in and it wouldn't be there when you drove out. The maid would identify which coat held the gun that killed Gina. Yours."

Lisa's hand searched for Mike's as she asked, "How could you count on the weapon being a gun?"

Tod answered, "We couldn't. Every method he chose so far had been different. I had men checking the food and drinks. Servants were alerted. When the maid informed me about the revolver, my men removed the actual bullets and replaced them with blanks.

"When Charlie called to tell me that you, Jarvits, were picking up Howard Stacey because his car was on the fritz, I had his automobile checked. At dinner I got a call saying the car was in first-rate condition. Howard had you pick him up to be absolutely certain which raincoat was yours.

"He hoped to get away with the revenge motive slapped on you. Mrs. Langley received an anonymous call that said you were out for revenge because of Dorothea. If anything happened to her, you'd be a prime suspect."

"And," cut in Charlie, "that letter you wrote, Mike – to Dorothea. The missing one? Howard got a hold of it. In time, I think, it would have turned up at headquarters. Further proof that you had a damn good motive."

Dolly quizzed: "But, Charlie, why the museum murders? Ullman— Carter—Gina's?"

"May I?" asked Charlie of Tod, who waved graciously, like the second member of a vaudeville team.

"Take it a step at a time. When the city's old museum shut down in deference to Gina, Howard automatically went onto Gina's payroll. He had no more business in a museum of that type than Buffalo Bill. He had a family name, but nothing else. He knew it. In the museum he had position. I got a fine glimpse of his mania for position the other day at lunch. He was afraid of you, Mike. Afraid of your knowledge and ability. Of your influence with Mrs. Langley. Somehow you had to be gotten out of the way.

"Mr. Jenckes established the fact that no one knew about the bequests in the will regarding the disposition of Gina's paintings. Yet Howard Stacey did."

"The day the museum opened," Charlie continued, "I complimented him on the collection and he said, 'Once the museum has Gina's collection. . .' Days later in casual conversation Mrs. Langley informed me that she had no intention of parting with the works, consequently Howard must have known they'd come on her death. Who could have known they'd come on her death. Who could have told him? Hank Ullman, obviously. They were friends. Perhaps it slipped out. Ullman had to be gotten out of the way, since, in time, he would remember that he told Howard about the will's contents."

Dolly asked quietly, "How did you discover about the paintings?"

"I got on the track thanks to something Carter Aubery said before his fake suicide. He said that it was in his will that his collection went to Gina, and vice versa. I thought—if his collection goes to Gina on his death, where does Gina's go if she dies? A visit to Mr. Jencke's office gave the answer – I – I – looked through some papers I wasn't supposed to see. The entire collection went to the museum, which, of course, passed on to the city, Howard as director. New municipal museum with an art collection worth several million dollars. But to accomplish all this, Howard had to move fast once Mike told him he was planning to resign. If you, Mike, did this it would mean you didn't give a hoot about revenge, and the whole scheme would fall apart. You had to stay on long enough for him to do away with Gina. What we had to do was force his hand. That's why we announced Mrs. Langley's departure. He had no choice."

Patting Mike's hand, Lisa asked, "What was he screaming when the police took him away?"

Charlie paused thoughtfully, then replied, "Position. He was screaming that he had position."

The door to the room opened and Juan, followed by two maids, each holding trays of food, entered. Gina followed along.

"Everyone must eat something before dawn," she said. "An ancient custom."

No one had heard of the custom, but they ate something anyway.

Tod said, "There are some odds and ends that have to be taken care of, but they'll keep."

Lisa and Mike remained seated, holding hands, talking softly like lovers in the dark. They were both smiling.

"I want to thank you for your cooperation, Mrs. Langley," said the police official. He took a swallow of coffee.

"Delighted to do the performance. Delighted. To be sincere, Howard Stacey was never a favorite of mine. Poor, poor, Michael."

Jarvits looked at Gina. She was grinning.

"When I fainted I do believe your heart skipped a beat or two."

"I won't deny that."

"Naturally, I didn't actually faint. What happened, Mike, was that I suddenly had the sensation I was back before the cameras. This room was the set. Shots rang out. I enacted a death scene. Brief. Much too brief for good effect, but convincing. I *was* convincing?"

Waking, Mrs. Crowley began to applaud from her chair.

"Howard who?" she asked.

The first hints of dawn, like wide golden fingers spreading out, colored the buttes. They would be back at the Shadows in a few minutes. For now, they were quite alone on the highway.

"About Dorothea," Dolly said, "is she one of the odds and ends to be tidied up?"

"I think as far as Tod is concerned, Dorothea Darnell left town some time ago. No one has put in a missing persons report; technically, it's no business of his."

"I see," she replied quickly. "Technically, technically. My, but that's a useful word, isn't it?" She didn't wait for him to answer, inquiring: "And Jerry Cox?"

"Tod tells me Mr. Cox has found Southern California very much to his liking. In fact, Tod suggested he stay there – indefinitely."

Again, "I see."

Charlie kissed his wife on the forehead.

"Charlie, how did you guess Howard in the first place?"

"Mrs. Crowley said she had called down to the museum to tell him everything was taken care of at Dreamy Pastures—"

"And?"

"But Mike said he never got any message. Remembering how often she confused you with Lisa and Mike with me, it was simple enough to guess that 'the man at the museum' who answered the phone wasn't Mike Jarvits, but the 'other' man who used the office – Howard Stacey. He now knew all about Dorothea's burial. This knowledge, plus knowing what was in the will, must have given him the idea. Soon after, the phone messages started."

Dolly nuzzled close to her husband, "I admire your cleverness. *Ugh*, that awful man. Trying to kill you, too. With scorpions, no less."

Guiltily, Charlie said, "Oh, *that*."

"Oh, that? You make it sound so unimportant. You could be dead."

"I took that specimen to Tod. So the lab could check it out."

"And?"

"Seems it wasn't a scorpion at all. Something called a pincher bug. They look alike but that's all. I -- I felt rather foolish."

"No scorpion?"

"No scorpion."

"Home to New Hampshire tomorrow?" she asked, running her hands over her lovely dress.

He nodded.

"Well, you may not be the world's best detective when it comes to scorpions, but I've one consolation about you."

"What's that?"

"A man who'll let his wife keep a dress like this can't be all bad."

About the Author

Tim Kelly (1931-1998) was a prolific and successful American writer, with more than three hundred plays to his credit. His works (which include comedies, dramas, one-acts, mysteries, melodramas, children's shows and musicals) have been performed by New York's Student Ensemble Theatre, Aspen Playwrights' Festival, the Seattle Repertory Company, and countless other theatres around the world. A television and screenwriter as well, Kelly wrote episodes of *The High Chaparral* and the cult films, *Cry of the Banshee* (1970) and *Sugar Hill* (1974). With the notable exception of the western novel *Ride of Fury*, Kelly did not focus his creative attentions on books. *The Museum Murders* (originally called "Paint Me a Murder," under his favorite pen name Vera S. Morris) was completed in 1959 and not released until this BearManor Media edition, fifty years later.

www.ingramcontent.com/pod-product-compliance
Lightning Source LLC
Chambersburg PA
CBHW072355030726
47505CB00014B/1833